THOMAS & JANUARY

FISHER AMELIE

Fisher Amelie

http://www.fisheramelie.com/

First Edition: June 2012

Printed in the United States of America

FOR REBECCA,
BEST FRIEND, SISTER, INSTIGATOR OF
SHENANIGANS, FELLOW HUMORIST,
AND ALL AROUND BAD ACE.
I LOVE YOU.

CONTENTS

THOMAS
&
JANUARY
GUITAR
music
Hip Hop
DISCO
COUNTRY
classical
A star
I
MUSIC
YEAH
WOW
RADIO
POP

Chapter One

First Day of My Life

Thomas

People crossed the street when they saw me. I'm not really sure why that was. I mean, okay, I might have looked a bit intimidating if I was being truthful with you. I'd changed since New York. New York represented a life that wasn't real, not truthfully, anyway. No, New York was the "young, immature, in love, idiot" side of Tom. The "Tie-Dye Tom of New York City" didn't exist anymore. Tie-Dye Tom was dead.

But that's okay because the new Thomas was happy with the new him. Kind of. Not really. At least he no longer looked like a douche bag. Well, I suppose that depends on your definition of douche bag.

For instance, if a tall, somewhat built, asshole is a douche to you than you probably wouldn't have gotten along with the new Tom because that's what he was. The only thing not drastically different from the old me was my given name. That's about it.

A couple of weeks after Callum married Harper, I discovered that I was in love with one of my best friends, Kelly Simsky. The idea hit me when I picked the ladies up to deliver them to The Bowery. I saw her in all her spritely glory, five feet one inch, barely reaching my waist, Kelly Simsky. Kelly Simsky with her short blonde hair, the blonde hair that met her chin and would drag forward when she laughed. Kelly Simsky, the tiny nymph of an actress who would sway and leap into a room and bow when she left. That Kelly Simsky. And damn, did I have it bad. I was forced to face the truth *just* about the time she met Carter Williams.

Speaking of douche bags. *Carter Williams.* Perfect Carter Williams with his perfect effing teeth, his perfect effing vocabulary, his perfect effing money, and his perfect effing sincerity. God, I hated that guy. He was my polar opposite in everything. Educated, born with money, and in possession of the one girl I wanted more than anyone. Perfect. Effing. Carter. Willams.

When Cherry and Charlie married, the band, *my* band, The Ivories, disbanded. I was pretty upset, but it was time. I knew it. We'd been at it six years with little interest from labels. We had a massive following, but as we all know, that doesn't get you signed, and there's only so many nights you can play for a measly five hundred dollars before you get bored with your band, no matter how awesome they are.

But that didn't mean my band didn't remain my family. No, it just meant we would have to find a different reason for hanging out on Friday and Saturday nights. And we did, but when Carter Williams began his ridiculous infiltration into my extended family, I was less than thrilled because that would mean I'd have to watch him lay hands on Kelly, but it was okay, because I was just biding my time until Kelly kicked Trust Fund to the curb, until she realized I was the one she was supposed to be with.

But that didn't happen. No, in fact, six months later Kelly's ring finger was dressed with the biggest freaking diamond I'd ever seen and that's when I'd lost my chance. So when my friend Jason from Seven Seas, one of the biggest record labels in the United States, offered me a chance to move to Austin for a year as a talent scout, I jumped at the opportunity. Hell, I leaped at the chance.

In Austin, I immersed myself in the culture and that's what it was, a culture, and a beautiful one at that. God, I loved Austin. It was weird. So weird with amazing barbecue and it was made for me.

Scouting bands until late at night, I'd still wake early not able to sleep because I wasn't over Kelly and she haunted my every thought, including my dreams. I'd hit the gym for a few hours, then return home to my apartment, ready to see more bands and repeat the entire process day after day...after day. For an entire year I did this, aside from one *tiny* indiscretion. Needless to say, I was an expert at finding awesome bands. I was also built like a freaking brick house.

Which is why people crossed the street when they saw me coming. Well, that and the fact I didn't wear a color on my body that couldn't be confused with night. Layers, that's what I felt comfortable in. Dark tees, black jersey hoodies, dark jackets, and I wore these together. Anything that would help me keep the hate in, along with black boots heavy enough to weigh me back down to this earth, preventing me from drifting off into insanity. I buried myself in my hair too, kept it at my jaw, as well as on my jaw. Camouflage. "Nobody look at me. I'm too busy being in pain." And I wanted the hate. I reveled in it, actually. I felt powerful and dangerous and pissed off, a perfect combination to intimidate the bands around me.

Soon, I had a reputation for being the guy with which one did not screw with. I also grew the reputation for being the scout you went to when you wanted to be taken seriously because I lived, breathed, and slept music. It was my only refuge from the hate I was drowning in and the only thing that kept the small sliver of flame that was the old Tom. I wanted that to burn slightly, to keep it around just to remind me of what I never wanted to go back to.

I was Thomas Eriksson, talent scout for Seven and scorned in a one-sided love. An amazing job and a worthless state of mind.

January

"It's time to pack your room, January. You've procrastinated enough even for me."

"Uh, Janet?" Janet's my mom. None of us were allowed to call her mom because the word "mom" was "intimidating" and she wanted her kids to be able to freely go to her and tell her anything. Most of us called her Mom anyway just to bug her.

"Yes, my love?"

Pull the Band-Aid. "I'm not going back."

My mom dropped the pan of tofu peanut butter cookies she was carrying to the table to cool.

"Excuse me, January?"

"I said, I'm not going back to Berkeley."

Janet grabbed the cracked linoleum countertop to balance herself. One of her signature dramatic moves that may have worked spendidly on me as a kid but held no real effect on me now that I was accustomed to nineteen years of her theatrics.

"Ralph! *Ralph*!" She called to my dad from the kitchen.

I heard a slow moving almost sarcastic shuffle from Dad's office to the entrance of the kitchen.

My parents were what you'd call made for each other. Mom and Dad met in college, ironically at Berkeley, and fell in love. They married, had ten kids, starting with me, January, and lived hectic lives of protests and pro bono law work all while towing us ten behind them. I loved them more than life itself, which is probably why I didn't have the heart to tell them that I was an anti-government, borderline anarchist. I felt like the less government was involved in my life, the better, because I'd seen firsthand what it did from the programs my parents supported. I'm not sure what my parents saw in government, but they were in love with it. Again, didn't have the guts to tell them that. Heart attacks are one of those things best left unprovoked.

"Repeat what you've told me, young lady! Tell him what you told me!"

I took a deep breath and steadied myself. "I'm not going back to Berkeley."

Janet sucked in a squeal and my dad fell into the chair next to me at the kitchen table.

"Now, *January*, explain to me why you're not going back?" he asked.

Another deep breath. "I'm not having fun there." Janet went to the sink to clean because that was what she did when she felt overwhelmed or wanted to slap one of us or both. "Cleanse the violent tendencies," she'd always say. Kind of liked that one.

"Fun," my dad asked incredulously. "It's Berkeley, January. Berkeley! Speak to me, love. Tell me why you don't want to return."

"I just want to write my music, Dad. I don't do well with structure."

Janet turned back around, seemingly calmer, and

sat next to my dad across the table from me. "Oh, January, I fear you're finally going to kill me this time."

"Janet, stop being dramatic," I told her, rolling my eyes. "It's not the end of the world."

"You'll lose your scholarship! A full ride to Berkeley's Department of Music, Ralph! Gone!" She straightened her slumped posture and looked me dead in the eye. "How are we going to tell Grandma Betty?"

That was her last resort strategy. I knew she had topped off her desperate meter when she brought grandma into the conversation. That probably would have worked accept I'd already told Grandma Betty. In fact, she's the one who encouraged me to follow my dreams. The day I told her I wanted to learn the piano, she encouraged me. It was no different when I phoned her with my intentions to quit Berkeley. She always supported me. Always.

"Janet," I said, leaning over and grabbing her dish-gloved hand, "I'm not going back."

That night, I agreed to go to my friend Casey's show. I promised I'd help him fine-tune a few of his songs so he could be ready for ACL in September in exchange for use of his couch since my parents kicked me out with a "have *fun.*" I was surprisingly unworried about my predicament. I knew something would come up for me. I had a gut feeling.

"What's up, doc?" I asked Casey.

"What's up, baby girl?" Casey said, lifting me up and spinning me around. "Every time I see you, you just get more and more beautiful, January MacLochlainn. Still single?"

"Ha, ha, Casey. What are you playing tonight?" I asked, as he led me back to his makeshift studio, otherwise known as his garage.

"Thought I'd start with *Pampered Life*. What do you think?"

"That's a strong start. Show me your list."

I sat down at his keyboard as I read over his list. We spent most of the afternoon cleaning up his set, then stopped by The Salt Lick and ate before heading toward Stubb's where his band, The Belle Jar, was opening for Circumvent.

Word around town was a talent scout for Seven Seas would be there to check out Circumvent. I really wanted The Belle Jar to be at their best. They were just as talented, if not more so, than Circumvent but had only been an Austin staple for about eight months.

"That's him," Casey said, nudging my shoulder with his. He pointed toward a blond guy wearing all black, but I could barely see him through the people crowding him.

"Who?"

Casey looked at me like I was a fool. "The Seven guy, doofus. Come on, we'll get closer. Try to edge in on him. Can I use your body to get me noticed?"

"Oh, by all means."

"Thanks, buttercup," Casey said, ignoring the bite in my words and disturbing the top of my hair.

"You're an idiot, Casey."

"I love you too, January. Fix your hair, it looks like shit."

I rolled my eyes at him and ran my fingers through my hair. We hedged through the crowd to AWOLNATION's *Not Your Fault,* finally finding this mystery guy slumped over the bar, again, surrounded by twenty people hoping to get his attention. Let me clarify, the twenty *girls* trying to get his attention.

When we got close enough and I could get a good enough view of him, I was forced to stop short. My heart beat wildly in my chest. My tongue swelled in my mouth and my chest felt constricted. My blood rushed through my veins, heating up my face and neck. He was unbelievably gorgeous. My hand flew to my neck to hide the obvious red I knew was painted there, a telltale sign that I was *intrigued* by something. Casey knew about this little trait I held and never let it down when it made an appearance.

He was tall, taller than most everyone in that room. He rested his forearms on the bar in front of him, a pair of callused hands, giving him away as a musician, nursing a pint on the flat wood before him. His hair reached just below his ears, which he tucked behind, and his goatee was a little scruffier than I usually liked but then again, I'd never been attracted to an actual *man* before. Mostly, my silly crushes belonged to some fellow teenager and usually ended as quickly as they started. He was frightening yet compelling all at the same time. I felt like a moth to a flame. My hands itched to run my fingers through his hair and along his jaw line. My eyes were transfixed on his mouth.

Snap.

"Come on, redneck." I cringed. "Yeah, didn't think I'd see that, did you? Well, I did. Come on." But just as Casey reached him, the lead for Circumvent beat him to the punch. Casey retreated.

"What are you doing?" I asked him. "Go up there."

"Nah, I can't move in when Stephen's there. I'll have to wait."

"Pansy."

"Okay, *redneck*. Let's go catch up with the guys. You can help me tune my keyboard."

"Hardy, har, har," I said absently, not able to take my eyes off the scout for Seven. I didn't move though. No, I dumbly stood there, staring like an idiot. I watched his beautiful mouth and teeth as he made conversation with Stephen. I imagined my own lips meeting his...Casey surprised me by throwing me over his shoulders and started to walk away, briefly distracting the Scout and Stephen from Circumvent.

The blush I knew was staining my entire body by that point boiled to an unnatural heat, and I tried to smile at the both of them but found my stare burning solely through the blue eyes that belonged to the scout. He eyed me with a hard expression, my insides came unglued a bit in alarm but also a little bit in excitement. I was Dali's melting clock personified at that moment. I felt like burning wax down Casey's back.

Casey set me down backstage after an embarrassing walk through the bar, a walk where the scout's eyes never left mine until we'd rounded a corner. I was humiliated.

"Gosh damn it, Casey!" I said, slapping his shoulder repeatedly. My hits felt like being pelted with cotton balls apparently because Casey was red with laughter. "You made a fool out of me!"

"Oh, calm down, January. He probably won't even remember you. He lives in this scene, remember? Sees that kind of nonsense all the time."

"Thanks, that's very comforting." I dropped my voice an octave. "No worries, January," I mocked. "You're not memorable enough to remember. You're invisible."

Casey's face softened. "Oh, baby girl, I'm sorry," he said, hugging me closely. "You're right. I apologize."

"It's okay, idiot."

Casey hugged me tighter. "You know you're memorable, right?"

"Sure, sure," I said, fighting back stupid tears.

"No," he said, bringing me out from under his arms, looking at me with a pained expression. "I'm serious, January. You're one of the most beautiful women I know, inside *and* out. If I wasn't in love with Sunny, I'd be all over you like white on rice."

"Shut up," I said grinning and shaking my head. "Let's go *tune* your *keyboard*."

We walked to the band room The Belle Jar was readying for the show in and I helped the band learn a lot of the key changes we'd made that afternoon. When I left to join the crowd at the bottom of the stage, I couldn't remember a time they sounded better to me. They were going to knock the scout's socks off the way he knocked me out of mine.

I positioned myself up front next to Sunny and we linked arms.

"Did you see him?" she asked.

"Yes! My God, Sunny. I don't think I've ever seen someone sexier than that scout."

"Scout? I meant Casey, but now I'm no longer interested in whether you've seen Casey," she said, her eyes roaming the crowd around us. She pulled me closely. "Who is this scout?"

"Seven Seas has a scout here to see Circumvent."

"Oh yeah, Casey mentioned something like that to me."

I stared at her in wonder. "I swear, woman! This is a huge deal!"

"I know, I know! I remember now."

I rolled my eyes playfully at her. We talked for a few minutes before The Belle Jar began to set up their instruments at eleven, readying for the show.

"Be right back," I said. "I'm going for a water. You want one?" I asked Sunny.

"Nah, I'm fine."

"'Kay, save my spot, missus."

I ran toward the bar and stood behind a few people waiting to be served. I kept throwing a head over my shoulder to spot the scout. *I'm a freaking maniac! Why can't I get this guy outta my head? I need to focus!*

"What's your poison?" The guy next to me asked.

I smiled at him. "I don't drink. Still underage." I held up my black x-ed hands in proof. "I'm in line for water. Boring, I know."

This usually worked, but not with this guy.

"That's cool. What are you doing out here tonight?"

"Oh, I'm here for The Belle Jar. I helped them clean up a few songs for tonight's show. There's a Seven scout in the audience for Circumvent tonight and I want them at their best. They're brilliant."

"Very cool. So, you're a musician?" he asked as we inched closer to the bar. It was still ten feet away.

"Yeah, a pianist." I turned my head away and fought a private grin.

"What's so funny?" he asked, confused.

"Oh, nothing. I-well," I said, facing him, "it's just, I threw away a full scholarship to Berkeley for music to stay in town and help *other* musicians become successful. It just dawned on me how ironic that was. I find that hilarious."

"That *is*...funny," he said, not finding it funny in the least.

"I know it's not funny, ha-ha, it's funny, ridiculous."

"Ah, I see." He looked around a bit, decided he was

bored enough to continue the conversation and asked, "So do you like Circumvent?"

"Yeah, I mean, I wouldn't dare step on an Austin staple like Circumvent's toes but, yeah, they're okay."

"No, really, tell me. I don't know about them. First time seeing them, actually. Enlighten me."

I bit my bottom lip, contemplating ragging on this band that was merely okay. "You tell anyone I thought this, I'd have to kill you, capiche?"

"Lips are sealed," he said, leaning closer.

"Circumvent," I began, "have an incredible base which is fairly impressive, but I believe that's because of longevity mostly. Their talent is mediocre, their songs catchy but a bit too commercial, and their stage presence lacks. They're just, 'meh.' They lack the talent to really push themselves over the edge, to put them in a position to gain a national following." As I spoke, the guy was leaning closer and closer to me. He looked at me like he'd just noticed me. "What?" I asked.

"What are you doing for a living right *now*....?"

"Oh, sorry," I said. "I'm January."

"I'm Jason," the guy said, holding out his hand.

"Nice to meet you, Jason," I said, taking his hand before dropping it. "I'm, uh, currently unemployed," I said, laughing.

"Cool, cool. Don't go anywhere after the show, okay?"

"Uh, okay," I said, eyeing him strangely.

"I'm not a freak. I promise," he said. "Just hang around in the crowd after the show. I'll find you."

"Why?" I asked him as he stalked off outside, forgetting why he was standing in line.

"Trust me. It'll be worth sticking around for."

This equally intrigued me as well as frightened me but not enough that I wouldn't find out what it was all about.

After I got my water, I headed back up front and squeezed my way through the crowd back to Sunny's side, but she was nowhere to be seen so I stood lamely by myself. I didn't care that much actually because I wanted a good "seat" for The Belle Jar. I wanted to be near the stage because there was a chance I needed to help cue Will on bass as he kept missing his new entrance on their third song.

Pampered Life shot out like a rocket from the beginning and blanketed the crowd around me, making everyone stunned by the power of it. It wasn't long before everyone realized that The Belle Jar was a force to be reckoned with. I was so proud of them, riding high on their talent right along with them.

Seemingly out of nowhere, my breath was wrestled out of my chest when I saw *him* inch closer to the stage, a quiet towering figure, eyes intent on the stage. *Oh, God. Oh, God. Oh, God. Breathe, January. Breathe.* He watched The Belle Jar with rapt attention. As I looked on him, my feet pushed themselves closer on their own accord. I was being pulled toward him by an unseen force. I found my feet planted right next to him but couldn't bring myself to look up at him. He was too magnificent to behold, really. He smelled so delicious I could have eaten him with a spoon. He was all man, no boy in him at all. I peeked briefly at his hands and guessed he probably played the bass judging by the size and location of the calluses.

I wanted to take his hands in mine and study them for hours, rub my thumbs over the worn bits of skin and warm them with my touch. The attraction I felt for him was heady and nothing like I'd ever felt for anyone before. My eyes followed his heavily clad feet, up his worn jeans, and around his wallet chain. I froze, not wanting to take it further, not wanting to know what I'd do if I went any higher.

A minute passed before my gaze traveled over the little bit of wide leather belt exposed under his dark, weighty hoodie and jacket. My eyes stopped at his goatee and I felt his considerable stare on my own face. He'd discovered me, but I was too enthralled to be embarrassed then. I reached up and met my eyes with his. They pierced me like an arrow, those ice blue eyes.

I don't know what came over me. I couldn't help myself it seems, and I watched my right hand travel up his arm slowly, glide over his shoulder, hesitate at his neck, but push further past the boundaries of sane as the back of my fingers trailed over the line of his jaw. I was pulled into the incredible magic this guy possessed over me. His skin was warm and surprisingly soft. His eyes closed at the feel of my hand, his jaw clenched slightly. I was distracted as his chest pumped with each deep intake of breath.

He surprised me when he turned more fully toward me and reached down, deliberately threading both his hands through my hair and bringing his face closely to mine. He narrowed his eyes, his brows furrowed slightly, conflict written in droves in the lines of his face. He took a deep breath in through his nose, languidly closed his eyes and exhaled slowly.

Sluggishly, I brought his beautiful mouth to mine. He tasted of mint and a little bit of yeast from the beer I saw him drinking at the bar earlier. It was the sweetest, most delicious flavor I'd ever tasted and, God, I wanted more. There was no shame in my motions as I gripped the front of his hoodie in both my hands and delved my tongue deeper into his mouth. The kiss became feverish, dangerous, heated.

He moved one of his hands from my hair to the back of my neck and traced his fingers down to the small of my back, pressing me deeper into his chest and hips, inciting a slight moan from me which only spurred him on more.

Suddenly, his eyes shot open in realization. He broke it abruptly, pushed me away lightly and set me right on my feet. I felt bereft of something but didn't know what that something was. I didn't know this guy, didn't know his name, yet it didn't scare me or make me feel ashamed in any way. It felt right, so very right.

We both stared at the other deeply, panting from the exertion of our unbelievable kiss. I opened my mouth to speak but closed it, breathing deeper through my nose to control my nerves. Nobody had ever made me feel the way this stranger did. He was like electric fire on my skin. I needed to know his name but the silence between us seemed impenetrable, neither of us wanting to break the charged calm that separated us.

Unexpectedly, his eyes became hard, his stare admitting...*disgust*? His jaw clenched harshly. He turned and walked away from me into the crowd, leaving me alone with myself, alone with my thoughts. My eyes began to water as the final comprehension of what I'd just done washed over me in shameful realization. I blinked and a single tear came cascading down my cheek. I wiped it away just as I looked back up toward the stage, Casey's face held an expression of concern, but I smiled at him just as I signaled to the bassist to begin his new entrance. *Perfect timing*, I thought absently.

I was no longer interested in seeing the rest of the set nor willing to endure Circumvent's. I didn't want to wait for the guy Jason from the bar either. I wanted out of there. I was humiliated and shunned and an idiot. Self-inflicted bad decisions seemed to be at the top of my list that day. I shoved my way through the crowd and finally broke free at the back on the verge of a sob. I went left into the bar just as someone grabbed the back of my shirt. I tried to ignore it, but the person insisted I turn around, so I did, ready to give them a few choice words but discovered the guy from the bar standing in front of me.

"I told you to stick around," he said in a friendly tone.

"I know but I've gotta jet. Something's come up," I said vaguely, tensing my expression to avoid shedding the tears that wanted so badly to come flooding at that moment.

"No, you're staying," he said, ignoring me and offering his arm. I opened my mouth to tell him to screw off, but he gave me a look that shut me up. "Trust me, January," he whispered kindly. "You are not going to want to miss this."

"Fine," I said, a little peeved but more sad than anything. I took his arm and we worked our way to the edge of the crowd as The Belle Jar's set came to an end. The crowd went berserk. "Told you," I said to Jason.

"You're right. They were different and talented."

"I know."

"But I want to see Circumvent now. I want to confirm what you've said."

"Why?" I asked, furrowing my eyebrows in suspicion.

Jason's eyes lit up when he noticed someone behind me. "Ah, there you are," he said, physically turning me around to meet whomever he was talking to. My stomach dropped when I saw who he meant for me to meet. The scout from Seven. The asshole I kissed (who kissed me back!) and left me in the middle of a crowd. "January, this is Tom. Tom, this is the girl I was telling you about."

Tom's eyes grew sarcastic, his mouth tilted to one side. "You move fast, little girl."

My mouth dropped open in shock. "*Excuse me*?"

All earlier sensations of sadness left me in a whoosh and replaced with anger. I could work with anger.

"Nothing," he said, a soft snort escaping. "Are you seriously wasting my time with this, Jason?"

"I'm *not* wasting your time, Tom."

My hand balled tightly formed before I could grasp what I was doing. Circumvent began playing just as I was about to bring my fist into *Tom's* mouth but Jason stopped my hand from shooting forward. He dragged me closer to the stage and away from Tom. "Do you know Tom?" he asked in disbelief.

"No, I don't."

"Then why - You know what? Never mind. I don't want to know."

We listened to one song by Circumvent before Jason dragged me back toward Tom. We stood there, Tom and I, seething toward each other. I'd offended this guy somehow. Since the kiss was burned so elegantly into my mind, I couldn't put my finger on why he was so pissed. I may have started the whole thing but he kissed me back. Trust me, he kissed me back, hard and without reserve. *He has no reason to be so arrogant. So mean. So...so...so...ugh!*

"You're right," Jason said, bringing me out of my hateful thoughts.

"What?" Tom and I said in unison.

"January. She was right. Circumvent was mediocre, at best."

"So what?" Tom said shrugging. "We were here to see The Belle Jar, I told you that." This surprised me and my eyes widened briefly.

"I know, but January offered me an honest opinion about Circumvent that bewildered me. She knows what she's talking about, maybe as much as you do, Tom."

"Sure she did. She's just a talented, talented girl, isn't she?"

"That's it!" I said, ready to throw that punch yet again.

"Jeez!" Jason exclaimed, dragging my body against his to prevent Tom getting the beating I wanted to throw his way. "What happened between you two? Do you know her?" Jason asked Tom, ignoring my earlier answer.

"No."

"Then what the hell is up with you guys? You claim you don't know one another but you're at each other's throats. What? Did he hit on you, January, and you turned him down?"

We both turned beat red, my throat and face heating to that unnatural red, giving me away.

"Ah," Jason said, jumping to the wrong conclusion. I wasn't going to correct him, his scenario put me in a better light and shunned this guy Tom, but what surprised me was Tom didn't correct Jason, he just stared at me harshly. "Dude, January, if Thomas Eriksson hits on you, you let him down easy. He's got a broken heart the size of Montana."

Tom shifted uncomfortably in his place. "I don't know what the fuck you're talking about."

"Come on! It's obvious, dumbass. In New York you're one person, you jump at the chance to move to Austin, you change everything about yourself here. You've been screwed over. Bad, from what I can see."

I stood there, watching both of them exchange a conversation I could tell I wasn't meant to hear. Jason, realizing this, shook his head and turned toward me.

"Listen, January, Tom is a talent scout for Seven Seas. Ever heard of them?"

"I'm not a complete idiot," I answered.

"The jury's still out on that," Tom said under his breath.

"I'm Tom's boss," Jason said quickly, hedging my reaction. "Though, now I'm not so sure anymore." Tom shrugged as if it meant nothing to him, this dream job, making Jason sigh. "Anyway, I'd like to offer you a position at Seven."

"*What?*" Tom and I said together, again. We turned to each other in disgust, pissed that we picked the same word.

"Seriously?" I continued on. I couldn't believe it.

"Seriously. You'd have to move to New York, though. Can you swing that?"

"Of course. I'm free as a bird." Tom snorted, but I ignored it.

"Good, it's gopher work for right now, but eventually, with some grooming, you can start scouting with a veteran."

"Oh my God, thank you, Jason," I said hugging him in a moment of unprecedented girliness. Jason was genuinely surprised and I felt a little embarrassed, my neck turning beet red.

"It's cool. I want you at this address," he said, handing me a business card, "in two weeks. It doesn't pay shit but neither does scouting, just ask Tom here." He smiled but the smile fell when we looked on Tom. "Uh, anyway, it's worth it. You've got an in with the execs and if you play your cards right, you can make some pretty decent cheese in time. Plus, it's a cool gig for musicians like yourself."

"So awesome. Thank you, Jason. I'm stoked."

I shook Jason's hand excitedly and told him I'd see him in New York in two weeks. I didn't even acknowledge Tom, turned and headed for the stage and let the crowd swallow me up, but somehow I felt Tom's stare, heavy and hot on the back of my neck and I clenched my hands.

Don't turn around. Don't turn around.

I turned around and there he stood, his eyes practically undressing me and I shivered from his hard stare. *What do you want me from me?* I begged him silently. I wanted him, this stranger, to want me as badly as I wanted him. I wanted him to part the crowd around me, scoop me up and drag me back to his car. I wanted his hands on my neck, my hair, my back, my body. I wanted his lips on mine. I wanted him with a fierceness I didn't find ladylike. I also wanted to sock him in the throat. *What is happening to me!*

His labored breath was visible from the twenty feet away I stood from him and when he was done perusing my body, he turned away in obvious disgust. *Gah*! My body shivered in reaction to his scrutiny. Even his stare set me on fire. *What is wrong with me?*

I shook my head and turned to meet The Belle Jar backstage. It didn't matter. In two weeks, I'd be living in Jersey with Grandma Betty and commuting back and forth to the city that never sleeps and as far away from this guy as I could get.

New York City, here I come.

Chapter Two
Something You Misplaced

Six months later....

Thomas

Jason signed The Belle Jar almost immediately which made me unusually happy, but that wasn't because I felt guilty about screwing over their friend, January. No, it was because they were a genuinely talented band and they were going to make the label millions, therefore making me indispensable. It wasn't because I thought about the kiss I'd shared with January more than I thought about Kelly lately or that I found January to be the hottest chick I'd ever seen. No, it was for the band. The band.

Even if I *was* into January, which I'm not saying I was, because she was a virtual stranger, she was over seventeen-hundred miles away in New York City, ironically trading places with the old me it seemed. Jason talked about her nonstop, which made me extraordinarily uncomfortable. He teased me incessantly about how she turned me down and about how she blew through the label like a perfumed tornado when she arrived, impressing everyone and solidifying her as a label necessity. Oh, and that apparently she was dating the guy who delivered everyone's *mail*? *Seriously, January? That guy doesn't even shower*!

A year into Austin, Jason rung me to tell me to pack my bags. The Belle Jar's debut CD, *Pick Your Poison, Miss Smith* went platinum and the label was throwing a party. Also, he said I wouldn't be coming back to Austin. Supposedly, I'd impressed Seven with my recent picks lately and they were sending me overseas. Dude, I was incredibly pumped and couldn't believe my luck. It was a dream come true for me. *Now, if I can just endure Kelly's presence, just long enough to hop a plane over the Big Blue and leave her memory behind. Yeah, you're running from Kelly, dude. Kelly.*

"Oh, God," I said under my breath as I picked up my luggage at the carousel and began the descent down the long corridor to catch a cab.

At the end, near the doors, stood Cherry, Charlie, Callum, Harper, and the rest of the gang, including Jason. Just to the right stood a bouncing Kelly on the arm of Carter. My stomach plummeted but not at the sight of Kelly, which shocked the hell out of me. No, it was because my eyes kept searching behind Jason for *January*, of all freaking people. *January!*

Marty held up a huge sign that read, "Mister Thomas Eriksson, Big Shot and All Around Badass." I dropped my bags and held out my arms. She ran to me and I picked her up, spinning her around, before setting her down and hugging all of my extended family.

"Love the sign, M," I told her, squeezing her

shoulders.

"You're welcome."

"So, my place or yours?" I asked everyone, inciting a cheer.

"Ours," Charlie said, gesturing to Cherry, as we all began to fall out the door, chatting amongst ourselves, excited and full of mischief.

"How've things been around here?" I asked for the millionth time that week when Jason and I got a few feet ahead of everyone.

"Dude, you keep asking me that and I told you, everything's cool. Is there something in particular you're worried about? Because Europe is a done deal, my friend. I've got your tickets all ready in my office. Chill." He eyed me warily before it dawned on him. "Oh, shit! It's the girl, isn't it?"

"What girl?" I feigned...badly.

"You've still got it for January MacLochlainn, don't you? She is hot as shit, Tom, but what about the one responsible for this wardrobe malfunction you've got going on?" he teased. I peered over my shoulder at Kelly, surprised that I sort of forgot she was behind us. Jason looked as well and nodded discretely. "Ah, I see."

"No, it's not like that anymore." I shook my head in disbelief at that revelation. "I guess I just needed time."

"Then, what, dude? I'm confused. You've been in my business hardcore lately and I'm curious as shit."

I sighed deeply. "It's nothing, man, really. I'm at a crossroads in my life, I guess. I've got this, though." I grinned. "Come on," I said, wrapping my arm around his neck and nudging his head. "Let's go get shit-faced."

"Cool."

The reason I'd been harassing Jason, it seemed,

though I wasn't aware of it until he'd enlightened me, was because I was fishing for information about January. There, I said it. I wanted to know more about this girl, the girl who infected my thoughts with the insane kiss she also polluted my dreams with. I convinced myself that she wasn't as beautiful as I imagined her to be, that she wasn't as sexy as I conjured her up to be. I knew then that I'd have to visit the label, and soon, to see for myself. Remind myself that she didn't affect me as much I thought she did, that I dreamed her up to help me get over Kelly. I was grateful for that little fact but needed to free all ties to her . I was ready to move on.

Then I remembered she'd probably be at The Belle Jar's Platinum Party the following night. In the car ride to Charlie's, I sat quietly staring out the window. It felt so good to be home again, but it wasn't too long before I began to wonder what she'd wear to this party, if she'd wear her long dark brown hair up or down, if her ears were pierced or not, whether she was still dating the mail guy. *Get a grip, Thomas*! I ran a hand down the front of my face before turning my attention to the car conversation.

I thought my distracted mind escaped the notice of all but when I caught Cherry's gaze, I knew she saw right through me. She narrowed her eyes at me.

"Callum, baby, switch places with me," she said. Callum kissed his wife deeply, making me think about January again, before moving to shotgun.

"Spill, Tommy. What's up with you? Aren't you happy to be home?" she asked. She was the only one allowed to call me Tommy. I didn't feel like I was ten years old the way Cherry said it.

"Of course, Cherry Bomb. I will never be able to be away from you guys for that long again," I said honestly, hugging her close.

"Then why the long face, kemo sabe?"

Quick, think of something. "It feels bittersweet," I said. Not a total lie. "I'm leaving for Europe in just a few weeks."

"Oh, Tom, you'll only be gone for the same. It's okay," she said, snuggling closely into my side. I wrapped my arm around her shoulder and squeezed, happy to be near my friends again.

That night we all got sloshed on wine and good food. The group sat around telling stories of the shenanigans I'd missed since my last visit and I almost died laughing hearing them.

"This is a refreshing side," Jason said to me as we both settled into chairs on Charlie's patio.

"What do you mean?" I asked, my bottle resting on my knee.

"When you're with these people," he said, gesturing through the window, "you're a different person, Tom."

"I'm not," I said, but even I knew that was a lie.

"Sure," he answered. "So, I invited January tonight."

"*What*?" I said, sitting up a bit, looking over my shoulder.

Jason smiled widely. "No, but I think I just figured out why you've been so effing crazy lately."

I shook my head denying it before he'd even spoken another word.

He ignored me. "She'll be at the party tomorrow, you know that?"

"I figured she'd be," I said, trying to sound absent. I avoided eye contact. "She's good friends with Casey Donigan."

"Yeah, she is, but she's also kind of responsible for the party arrangements. She practically did all the prep for it. She's a cool chick."

"That's cool," I said, trying to be that very word, but the curiosity was killing me. "So, uh," I said taking a swig of beer, "is she still seeing that dude from the mailroom?" *Smooth.*

"No, actually, she's *free as a bird,*" he said, borrowing a line from her the night I'd made a fool of myself.

"Oh, cool."

"God, you idiot. Shall I just set a date at the church then because you're clearly infatuated with her. Just bite the bullet, Tom. Damn, never thought I'd have to say that to you of all people."

"Shut it, Jason."

"Yeah, yeah," he said, lifting up his six pack and heading for the window.

"Finally," I said under my breath.

Jason was right. I was clearly infatuated with her, but that was all. We shared an amazing kiss that nearly flayed the skin from my bones from the sheer razor-sharpness of it, but that was it. I was attracted to her but didn't want to get to know her. Besides, say, for hypothetical sake, I even wanted to get to know her, I was headed to Europe soon. I didn't have time to get to know her.

Saturday night was The Belle Jar's platinum party. That morning, I woke on Charlie's patio on one of his ridiculous chairs, my back aching like no other. I peeled myself through the window and stood straight in their dining room, stretching my body to rid myself of the kinks.

"Tom?" I heard from the kitchen.

"Yeah, Cherry. It's me."

"Where the heck did you come from?" she asked , laughing and rounded the counter.

"You left me out there all night. Some friend you

are," I teased.

"Yeah, well, maybe you shouldn't have fallen asleep out there, goofus."

"I'm out of here," I said, yawning.

"What? Why? Stay for breakfast!"

"Nuh uh. I've got to get ready for this party tonight. You guys are coming, right?"

"Now, that was a dumb question," she teased. "When have any of us denied the chance to dance and party, my friend?"

"I suppose that was dumb," I said, straightening a stack of papers on her bar top. "See you," I said, kissing her cheek and heading out the door.

My apartment was a few blocks down from Charlie and Cherry's. I'd lived in Austin for a year, yeah, but the label still paid my rent here, and I had a roommate who didn't mind getting the apartment all to himself. I'd dropped my bags there earlier when he wasn't home but could hear him in the kitchen when I walked in.

"Tom?" I heard from around the foyer hall.

"Yeah, it's me."

"Good," my roommate Matt said, meeting me halfway. He gave me a slap hug. "Thought I'd have to bring out the big guns," he joked.

"You got a gun?" I asked.

"No - I...never mind. Come in, asshole. Haven't heard from you in a couple of weeks. What's new, man?"

"Oh, nothing. Got a sweet deal from the label a few days ago. Going to Europe to scout."

"Damn," he said, his cereal-laden spoon stopped halfway to his mouth. "That's cool."

"Yup," I said, heading toward the room I hadn't seen in a while.

"I had Sal clean in there. That cool?"

"Of course," I said, before closing the door behind me.

My room was in perfect order and exactly as I'd left it. I brushed my teeth in my attached bathroom, threw on my workout clothes and headed out into the New York streets to run a few miles. Working out in New York was definitely different than working out in Austin. The air was very different and I was finding it hard to adjust. I went five miles before turning around and heading back home, unable to go further. In Austin, I'd run six before turning back. It probably didn't help that I drank so much the night before. I'd come to be a lightweight. I only drank socially and usually had only one or two beers but that night I'd gone a little overboard.

At home, I showered and tucked a towel around my waist before heading for my suitcases and dragging out a pair of boxers. I unpacked, putting everything up so I could see what I could scrounge up that was decent enough for the party. I was spoiled in Austin. It was such a laid-back city, there was no dress code for things like this.

I couldn't find anything, then decided I didn't care. I threw on a pair of jeans and belt, stuck my wallet in my back pocket, making sure the chain didn't hang weird, then picked a black t-shirt and hoodie and threw my green military jacket over that. I cleaned my boots up a bit and threw those on as well. Since I'd woken so late at Cherry and Charlie's, and unpacking had taken forever, I'd lost track of time. When I looked at my watch, I was actually fifteen minutes late.

"Shit! Nine-fifteen?" I asked no one.

I rushed out the door, not because I was in a hurry to see what January looked like after all these months or to see what she thought of me. No, I was excited to meet my friends. Yeah, that's it. I hailed a cab but when the cabbie asked where to, I couldn't tell him. I'd forgotten to ask Jason. I'd flipped my cell open and rang him.

"Yo!"

"Jason, where's this party at?"

"The Bowery."

Seriously? Did she do this on purpose?

"The Bowery," I told the cabbie.

The Bowery was special to me for lots of reasons. I used to perform there all the time with my band, The Ivories, and Callum married Harper there. It was *our* place.

"See you there," I told Jason and hung up.

The cab pulled up in front and I could hear the dull bass from the club beat into the street. My stomach dropped a little and my heart jumped in my throat. *Just go in there and chill out.* I walked up to the doorman.

"Name?" He asked.

"Thomas Eriksson," I said.

The guy flipped through the list. "Sorry, you're not on here." His eyes lit up. "In fact, your name's under the 'Do not permit under any circumstance' list."

"Is that a joke? What kind of list is that?"

"Exclusively yours, it seems. Your name is the only one under it." He smiled smugly.

"You're screwing with me."

"No, sir."

"Get Jason Barrett out here."

"I'm sorry, but it says right here..."

"I know what it says. Just get Jason Barrett here."

"I apologize, sir, but we can't," the bouncer said, stepping in, enjoying his position of authority a little too much.

"Screw this," I said, reaching for my cell. I flipped it open and dialed Jason.

"Yo!" I barely heard through the blaring music.

"Jason, come to the door!" I yelled.

"What!" he screamed.

"Come to the *door!*"

He hung up and I just hoped he'd heard me correctly. Five minutes later, Jason walked out and signaled for the bouncer to let me in.

"What was that all about?" he asked.

"January," I seethed.

"Oh, hoo, *hoo,*" Jason laughed. "That is rich."

"You're gonna let her get away with that?" I asked, incredulous.

"Hell yeah I am! She burned you and she didn't even have to be there. That girl, I swear," he said, shaking his head.

When I finally glimpsed into the ballroom, I couldn't believe my eyes. The music pumped loudly, which wasn't unusual, but what took my breath away was the swathes of billowy cloth that hung from the ceiling over our heads, giving the entire room an ethereal feel. I refused to give her credit for that. *Probably someone else's idea.* Jason had abandoned me, distracted by an issue at the front again, leaving me to my own devices.

That little punk ass. I searched the floor for her. I had a few choice words to lay into her. I wanted to be cured of her poisonous claws and burning me like that was one way to do it, thanks to her delightful butt. My eyes scanned the room around me. I almost hoped she was on the dance floor. I imagined myself dragging her off by her hair to the edge. *No, too Neanderthal.* She wasn't near the bar nor anywhere near the throngs of girls in the line for the restroom. I finally spotted her on stage, leaning over the DJ's tables.

But spotting her held the opposite effect I wanted it to have on me. In fact, all vexation I previously felt for her dissipated into puddles at my feet. *Damn it!* She *was* as beautiful as I'd remembered. More so, in fact. She was bent over the tables, the hem of her short skirt riding slightly up her muscular thighs. Her long dark brown hair was down and cascaded over her shoulder, shielding her face. I hated how much I liked that she'd worn it that way. She'd curled it into waves and I thought back to how those strands felt sifting through my fingers.

She righted herself and laughed at something the DJ had said, making a slow jealous burn seep into my chest. My breath caught at the sight of her. *Damn it!* She turned and somehow found me at the edge of the dance floor. She narrowed her eyes at me, a cold stare seeping through the people around me hit me like an atom bomb and causing my stare match hers.

She walked with purpose off stage left, making a beeline straight for me. The heated anger emanating off this girl parted the waves of people dancing like the Red Sea. The cleared path in front of her gave me an excellent view of her swaying hips for which, I feel sad and pathetic to have to admit, I immediately imagined pinching between my thumbs and fingers.

"Hello, Mister Eriksson," January said, overly polite. Any stranger walking by would mistake it for the saccharine it appeared to drip, but I knew it for the acid it really was.

"Miss MacLochlainn."

She stood comfortably in front of me, her hands laid gently at her sides, one hip cocked. "I see you got in."

"I did, thank you."

Her eyes briefly flashed something wild. She was trying to bait me. I wasn't falling for it and that was obviously pissing her off. *That* made me smile.

She eyed me strangely for a moment. "Huh. You do have teeth. Lost that bet." She stood a bit taller at the insult. "Listen, if you need anything and I mean *anything*, don't hesitate to ask. It's why I'm here," she said sarcastically and began to walk off. *Don't let her have the last word, that would be too mature.*

"Oh, I believe I've had about all I could possibly want from you," I barely said, but it was enough to catch her attention.

She stopped, straightened, her hair shifted off her shoulders as she whipped back around and came stomping up to me like a five-year-old. I tried to fight the grin that spread across my face but couldn't.

"I'm sorry, did you say something?" she asked, a foot from my face. I ignored the way my pulse raced at her proximity.

"I apologize," I said, leaning in further. "I'll speak more clearly then. You couldn't give me anything you haven't already. You're quite the generous hostess, it seems."

And the facade finally breaks. "You've got a lot of nerve! You know that?"

I fell to the back of my heels, wrapping my arms in front of me.

"You kissed me back!" she continued. "I was there! I know when someone kisses me back and you *kissed me back*, Thomas Eriksson!"

I avoided eye contact, glancing to my right a bit, and noticed a waitress getting ready to pass with a tray of drinks.

"Excuse me, miss?" I said, leaning around the statue that was January. The waitress offered me the tray and I took a cold Heineken. "Thank you."

January's face and neck burned a bright red. At any moment, I suspected steam would start pouring from her ears.

I took a swig of beer before answering, still avoiding eye contact. "I didn't kiss you back."

She leaned into me, inches from touching me, making my blood pressure spike to unhealthy levels. "You did. I felt you did," she whispered. "Trust me, there's nothing you can do or say or even pretend that could convince me otherwise."

"You tell yourself whatever you need to in order to make you believe that, January, if it makes you feel better. Justify slutty behavior however you wish." She stumbled back, hit hard by my unfeeling words. I closed my eyes briefly. I immediately regretted hurting this virtual stranger. I felt physically ill at the lie. I didn't really feel that way, in fact. Truthfully, that girl just brought something out of me I couldn't control and it scared the shit out of me.

"You're an asshole," she whispered, her eyes glassy. She turned and stalked away toward the stage once more.

I reached for her but didn't reach far enough. Every second she walked away I felt too ashamed to apologize to her. I was a coward. I knew it. *Never too late to do the right thing*. I started walking her direction but noticed she'd walked straight up to Casey from The Belle Jar and started sobbing into his shoulder. *Shit! I* am *an asshole!* When Casey saw me coming, he sat January at the edge of the stage with his girlfriend Sunny and came at me like a bull and I was waving a red flag.

"Can I talk to you, dude?" Casey asked, fury built in his eyes.

I led him to a nearby table. "Listen," I began but he interrupted me.

"No, you listen," he said, incensed, "I don't care if you helped my band get to where it is, and I also don't know what the hell you and January have going on. Frankly, I find it odd because she claims she doesn't know you, but somehow you can make someone I've never seen cry in the three years I've known her, cry and trust me, she's had plenty of reason to. Now why, I ask you, is she over there bawling her eyes out?"

"There's no reason, truthfully. I owe her an apology. We...butt heads."

"Why?" he asked, his eyes narrowed.

"No reason. Haven't you ever met someone you didn't like?" *Or really liked but didn't want to?*

"I have but that person has never been January, for me or anyone else for that matter. What's wrong with you, Tom? January is literally the best girl I've met in my life and I've met a lot of girls in this business." He took a deep breath. "Seriously, January MacLochlainn is a freaking saint."

The guilt started weighing hard on my chest then. I was taking my pissed off nature out on a beautiful, innocent, amazing girl for no other reason than I didn't want to find her beautiful, innocent or amazing. I wanted my hate back. I stood up and squeezed Casey's shoulder.

"I'll apologize to her. I'm sincerely sorry for the shit I just pulled."

"Good," he said, calming down. "God, Tom, I always knew you were a bit of an ass, but I've never seen you do something so low."

"I know, dude. I'm ashamed. I'll go apologize right now."

I walked January's direction. She saw me coming and stood taller, not wanting me to see I'd affected her. She subtly wiped the tears from underneath her eyes, but it didn't help, they were still red, sending me down another shame spiral. I could do this. The old Tom could have done this with amazing ease.

"January," I said softly.

"Yes?" she asked coldly.

"Can I talk to you outside for a moment?"

"No."

"Please?" I begged her pathetically.

She sighed deeply. "I guess," she said, letting me lead her outside.

When we reached the sidewalk, I led her a little farther down away from the noise of the club, stopping right underneath a street light. The light bathed her head like a crown. *A saint,* Casey had said. "I'm so sorry," I said genuinely. "I didn't mean any of the shit I said."

"It's okay," she said a bit more warmly than her earlier tone, but she still refused to meet my eyes.

"No, it's not," I said, lifting her chin softly so her eyes would meet mine. "You're right, I'm an asshole. I've been one for more than a year and I never realized just how bad I'd gotten until I'd met you. You bring out this insane side of me for some reason, and although I'm still trying to decipher what that is exactly, I do want you to know I didn't mean a single word I said in there."

She was quiet for a moment, mulling over my apology. "You admit you kissed me back?" she asked, a small grin tugging at the side of her mouth.

I hated to admit it, but I knew I couldn't lie anymore. She'd know. "Yes, January. I kissed you back."

"I knew it," she said, a gleam in her eye. She abruptly turned from me and walked back to the club, abandoning me to the newly discovered harsh light of the street lamp.

"She played me," I said under my breath, shaking

my head at the ground. I smiled the widest, shit-eating grin. "She played me." *Probably wrong about that innocent part.*

Chapter Three

Betrayed by Bones

Thomas

A week later and I had yet remove extra space to see January since the party, which was just fine with me because the little wench had played me like a fiddle. As I was packing for Europe the next day, I heard my cell vibrate on top of my dresser. I scanned the caller ID and saw it was Jason.

"Yo," I said, tucking the phone between my chin and shoulder and continued to pack.

"Need you to come down to the label right now."

"Dude, are you kidding me?" I asked, grabbing the phone again. "I'm not exactly prepared for this trip."

"Just get down here," he said succinctly before hanging up.

I pressed end and leaned against the heavy wooden dresser, studying the phone, not sure why Jason needed me but feeling on edge at how short he'd been.

I threw on my hoodie and jacket, tucked my keys in my pocket and headed for the door. Downstairs, I hailed a taxi, worrying my lip the entire ride there. Jason was waiting on the street, smoking a cigarette when I pulled up next to him. I paid the fare and got out.

"What's up, man?" I asked him.

"Nothing, what's up with you?" he said, taking a last drag before putting it out with the toe of his shoe.

I nearly punched him. "Jason, you sounded like something was up. What's going on?"

"Oh, nothing," he laughed. "I'm just about to head out for the night, but I wanted to hear them deliver this news to you first. I was in a hurry."

"You're an idiot."

"Thank you. Coming from you, that's a slight compliment."

"What's going on?" I asked.

"Oh, you're just about to get planted on your ass is all. Excited? I am," he said, slapping his hands together and rubbing them together quickly.

"Jesus, what does that even mean, Jason?" I asked as we walked briskly to the elevator.

Inside, Jason leaned against the railing after pressing the button for the fifteenth floor. "Have fun at the party?" he asked breezily.

I joined him on the railing on the other side of the car. "Not really," I answered. I eyed him in the reflection of the doors. "Why do you ask?"

"Oh, no reason."

Shit. He definitely knows something.

The doors silently fell open and I followed Jason past the receptionist's desk, long abandoned for the evening, down the long corridor to the executives' suites, passing the large plaques of albums gone gold and platinum on the walls. I had a hand in half the bands' successes, which is probably the only reason they put up with me as well as paid me anything decent. A well paid scout was unheard of in this industry. And I knew it. I was nervous as hell that they were about to cut me loose, not that Jason would've been happy about that, which is why I was only *partially* nervous.

We entered the president of Seven, Peter Weathervane's, office a moment later. His massive corner office had a cool mid-century modern feel, courtesy of wife number three. His last wife decorated in an African motif after they'd returned from Safari. Apparently his wives couldn't leave any trace of the last, making me wonder what number four had in store for him.

"Tom," the man said, startling me. He was hidden behind a high back office chair, facing the city below him. He turned around slowly, a subtle smile gracing his face. "I'm glad Jason got you here. Sit down," he said, gesturing to the sleek leather chairs in front of his desk.

We both sat. "So, what's up Mister Weathervane?"

"Please, how many times do I have to tell you, Tom? It's Peter."

"All right, Peter, how've you been?"

"I'm doing well," he answered, standing up and walking to his bar. "Anything?" he offered. Jason and I both shook our heads. "I called you here because there've been some developments. Turns out, our R&D Rep (Relations and Development Representative) has decided to call it quits. I'm looking for a replacement."

I sat up in my chair a little, swiping the palms of my hands on thighs.

"Anyway," he continued, sitting back down with a straight whiskey, his usual. "We're considering you for the position."

I didn't get too excited. He'd said "considering" and that word means a hell of a lot when Peter Weathervane says it.

"I see," I answered. "Whom else is being considered?"

His eyes lit up a bit. "You were always quick, Tom. Jonah White."

Of course it was Jonah White.

Jonah White had been a friendly/unfriendly rival of mine from day one. He'd been doing this gig longer and he'd been pretty damn good at it, but I learned how to do it better. He was beloved by every single person within the label though, and that's why he was being considered as well. Plus, he knew the industry a little better than I did. He just didn't possess the ear I did and it was only a matter of time until I passed him up, I knew it. He knew it.

"He's good," I said, offering nothing else.

"I know," Peter said, goading me.

"I'm better."

"He doesn't seem to think so," he laughed.

"So what's the deciding factor?" I asked, shifting slightly.

"Europe," he said succinctly.

"I see. I'm game if he is."

"Already got the green light from Jonah."

"Cool," I said.

"Now, get out of here. I bet you haven't even packed."

I offered him a genuine smile and stood. I shook his hand and Jason and I left together toward the door.

"Three, two, one..." Jason said under his breath. I eyed him warily.

"Oh, and one more thing," Peter added, before lighting up a cigar. We stopped just outside his door. "January MacLochlainn will be shadowing you."

I knew my mouth must have hung open from the look Peter gave me, but he had shocked the hell out of me. Jason quietly shut the door behind us. I bent quickly to open the door, to assure Peter that she would not, but Jason held me back.

"Now, now," Jason said. "Don't be hasty. Do you really want to ruin any chance of a permanent position in a permanent city?"

I hesitated slightly but reached for the door again.

"Stop it, you idiot," he said, pushing me toward the elevator.

We rode in silence, a ridiculous grin plastered on Jason's face.

"What the hell is so funny?" I asked him, pissed beyond belief.

"Nothing. Like I've said all night, *nothing*."

I tossed and turned that night, unable to sleep thinking of the fact that I was going to have to share tight quarters with the minx from Austin, enduring her hellishly beautiful face and her sharp tongue. Why did life have to be so damn complicated for me lately? She was going to make it impossible to concentrate. I didn't want to have to train her, endure her, and fight for the position Peter was lording over my head, all the while running into Jonah at the festivals, particularly Paris' "Windmill Music Festival," I knew we both would immediately consider for new talent.

After a measly three hours sleep, I awoke groggily and extremely irritable. I showered, attempted to let the hot water seep away my terrible mood but it didn't work. I dressed in my usual attire, tossed my oversized canvas duffel bag over my shoulder and headed for the train. I sat relaxed on the train, listening to my iPod and shuffled through songs but stopped short when I heard a song I'd never put in my queue. I sat up a bit and listened carefully.

Neil Sedaka's *Calendar Girl* played, making me curse myself when the line "January, you start the year off fine..." rang clearly through my ears.

Damn it, Jason!

I took my cell out and began a text.

REALLY, JASON? HOW DID YOU EVEN ORCHESTRATE THAT? JUST REMEMBER, PAYBACK'S A BITCH

Five minutes later, my cell buzzed with the simple message.

HA HA HA HA HA

Jerk.

The airport was surprisingly packed for four a.m., but I still had no trouble whatsoever finding January. She stood a head taller than every woman there. She was also more beautiful than any other woman there. I approached her slowly before I noticed the equally tall asshole standing beside her. *Not the mailroom guy, though.* Still, jealousy burned through me with a vengeance, pissing me off even further.

"I will," I heard her say before hugging the guy fiercely around the neck. "I love you. I'll ring you when I get there."
The guy kissed her cheek before leaving her through the sliding doors. *Ha! A peck on the cheek! Sucker!*

That's when she noticed me and she checked her glassy eyes. She stood taller, her back erect, and followed me with cold, hard eyes.

"Tom," she gritted, the word polluted with hate. I involuntarily cringed.

"January," I said politely, trying desperately not to rock the boat.

We stood in line to retrieve our tickets.

"Are you two together?" The attendant at the end of the line asked us.

"No," January said with conviction just as I said, "Yes." I eyed her harshly. This would go a lot easier if she chilled.

"Just step up to one of the unmanned kiosks," the guy said.

I did and to my absolute shock, January followed. I ran my driver's license through the machine, answered a few stupid questions, and retrieved my boarding pass. I checked my bag and stood aside for January to do the same. She did but with absolutely no word spoken to me.

We walked in silence through security and all the way to the plane and sat on opposite sides of our gate's seating area. I watched as she worried her lip, flipped through a magazine, and returned a few texts. *No doubt to that asshole I saw outside.*

Watching her full mouth brought me back to that night at Stubb's, the feel of her hands threading through my hair, the taste of her lips against my tongue. I cautiously licked my lips as if I could still taste her. She drove me crazy in so many freaking ways.

I'd kissed a lot of girls in my life. Hundreds probably. It was the perk of being in a band. It wasn't until Kelly that I realized I didn't want that life anymore. At twenty-two, I'd admittedly grown old, a lifetime of experiences fulfilled by a sensory overloaded New York City. I was looking for something substantial by then, until she killed that dream for me by agreeing to marry someone else. Sure, I was over her and that still shocked me, but I realized something after Kelly, no one was worth feeling like shit for...not like that, ever. I'd resigned myself to loner-hood long before I'd met the kitten fiddling with the necklaces choking her throat. Damn January MacLochlainn and her intriguing face.

"Loading zones ones and two," I heard over the intercom. That was us. I stood and she followed suit, taking a long stride for each one of mine. We stood silently side by side but her carry-on carry-on was obviously too heavy for her because she kept struggling with trying to handle the awkward bag as well as her oversized purse. *God, what does she have in there?* Every step forward was an overexerted effort, so I took the carry-on carry-on from her without asking. She held fast to it as the line moved, but I refused to let her have it back. We stood there, silently fighting over her ridiculous carry-on until the guy behind us cleared his throat. I yanked it from her hands. She huffed and straightened her clothing, puffing her disheveled hair from her face. We boarded the plane without a single word. People probably thought we were both crazy.

Unfortunately, we were forced to sit coach because the label, although made of money, apparently didn't like to spend it. Row eight, seat B, loomed ahead of me like a dentist's chair. Seven hours of pure hell laid ahead of me.

"You can have the window seat," I said, gesturing to the inside seat. "I'll take the aisle." *Try to keep the peace.*

"No, I'd rather sit in the aisle, thank you."

I stuffed her carry-on above us then took a deep breath to compose myself. "Seriously, I don't mind giving up the window."

"And I told you, I don't want it," she gritted.

My blood was beginning to boil now. "January, I'm trying to be cool with you."

"I realize that and I said thank you but no thank you."

"Fine," I gritted back. I sat in the window seat, opened the plastic shade and watched the men below load our bags with the utmost care you'd expect those men to handle your bags. Yeah.

By the time the plane, took off, I was asleep.

January

Tom fell asleep before we even left pavement, for which I was grateful because I didn't want to have to explain to him my most inconvenient problem. I was allergic to traveling. Well, not allergic so much as just extremely susceptible to motion sickness. It didn't matter what I was traveling in, be it plane, train, or automobile. I had a genetic predisposition of ralphing everything in my stomach each time I barely set foot on any form of transportation. It's why I argued over keeping the aisle seat, I needed to have better access to the lavatory.

As soon as Tom drifted off, I swallowed down the motion sickness pills my doctor prescribed me with my bottle of water. These I only took when I would be able to sleep for hours because they made me sleepy as hell.

While I waited for the pills to take effect, I took out the tattered paperback I'd brought from home and settled into my seat but couldn't bring myself to bend the barely-there cover. I worried that my motion sickness issue would become just that, an issue for Tom. Scouting involved an astronomical amount of traveling, and although I knew this going into it, I wasn't going to let my little problem stop me from doing it. It was a once in a lifetime opportunity and the job was made for me. There was nothing I loved more than music. Music kept my heart beating, my mind clear and my soul deep.

Drowsiness took over and my head started to feel heavy on my neck. Before I knew it, my book had slipped from my fingers, tumbling to the floor at my feet.

Thomas

I vaguely remember falling asleep but I definitely remembered waking up. I was staring at the top of January's head, her long, silky brown hair laid arranged across my chest. She'd accidentally fallen asleep on me and I grinned at that. She'd flip her shit if she knew she'd done that. I studied it. There were red highlights throughout and it gleamed in the sunlight that shone through the window. I shut the window to keep myself from running my hands through it. I breathed deeply to keep myself in check, but that only magnified the problem because it kicked up whatever perfume she was wearing and my head began to swim.

I tried to shift her but she groaned. I was stuck. I dared not disturb her because I enjoyed this peaceful side of the girl I knew nothing about but somehow felt

I knew better than anyone else. I needed a distraction. I slowly reached for my iPod in my jacket pocket and brought it out. I put the buds in my ears and an old Dashboard came on. While *Where There's Gold* played, I tried hard not to let the lyrics remind me of the dreams I'd lost. I tried, but failed. Bitterness began to paint my thoughts with the poison only bitterness could infect with. Regret. Lots and lots of regret.

A few months before The Ivories disbanded, I knew it was over. Things were taking place that simply gave it away. Cherry started to miss practices to hang out with Charlie, not that any of us had cared, we all had things to do that seemed more important. Our songs suffered for it and our sizable following recognized it, so they simply stopped showing up.

I started to become obsessed with Kelly, making up excuses to hang out with her. This made Carter incredibly nervous, rightfully so, and she had to end our little private dinners and lunches and movies. I knew it wasn't right for me to take advantage of Kelly's naivety like that. I knew I was wrong, but I still felt an added cover of bitterness creep into my heart that Carter didn't want her to do as she wished. Another thin veneer of bitterness was added on top of my growing layers as well because it felt like she had started to feel the same way about me as I did for her. I knew if we could've had another month or so, she would've been mine.

That's when I took the Austin gig. I thought it would've helped me move on, find solace in a career worth taking solace in but being alone only magnified how much my heart had hardened and before I knew it, it'd turned to stony ice to keep from hurting so damn badly.

That's why I resented January so much. That night, that embrace, that *unbelievable* kiss cracked my carefully guarded, steeled heart. She reminded me of what I didn't want to remember wanting anymore. I didn't want to know the comfort of someone's touch or kiss. I just wanted to be alone, regardless of what that would cost my life because nothing was as costly, in my opinion, as a broken heart. Nothing.

January

I woke to the faint sound of Tom's iPod in my ear. *Damn, he's playing that loudly. Doesn't he know he's gonna remove apostrophe lose his hearing at that decibel?* I inwardly sighed. *Why should* you *care, January?*

Something felt off though. That's when I realized that he wasn't playing it loudly....at all. In fact, I'd only heard it so well because I was practically on top of his lap! My face and neck flamed red, of course, and I silently thanked God that my hair was fanned across my face, hiding my reaction. I smiled lightly. *Hmm, while I'm here...* I took him in. His chest was hard and wide and so incredibly warm. I inhaled deeply, making sure to keep my breathing even so it wouldn't give me away, and smelled his astonishingly yummy smell. Oh my Lord, he was built like an Abercrombie model. I felt it underneath the ridiculous layers of clothing he hid himself in. I wanted to lift his hoodie and run my fingers down his washboard abs. Then I panicked and adrenaline began to pump through my veins...because I was a drooler. I know, I know, not exactly the most ladylike admission but I was nonetheless. I carefully pressed my lips together to feel for excess moisture. Dry. *Thank God.*

It's time, January. I needed to pretend to wake and act astonished that I was laying across his chest *and* that I didn't enjoy it. If I was going to pull it off, I'd need to channel my inner Meryl Meryl Streep. I slowly stirred. *Good, you're doing good. Now, rise. Awesome. If I survive, I should get an Academy Award for this.* But when my eyes met his, my body had other plans. It flamed a bright red, crept right up my neck and colored my ridiculous face. God, how I hated that I had no control over this part of myself.

"Good morning, sunshine," he said sarcastically. "Have a nice sleep, did you?"

"Sorry," I said sheepishly, averting my eyes slightly. I caught the attention of a guy two rows up from me. He mistook my blush for being caught staring at him, which I wasn't, obviously. He winked and I rolled my eyes, making me blush deeper.

I noticed Tom eyed me carefully. "What?" I asked harshly.

"Oh, nothing, really."

"Seriously? *What*?"

"You can't help it, can you?"

"Help what?" I asked, shrinking into myself.

"That," he said, gesturing subtly toward the idiot two rows up.

"What exactly are you implying?" I gritted out. What was it about this guy that brought out the cynical in me?

"I'm not implying anything, January. I'm simply making an observation."

"Please, enlighten me, Tom. What exactly did you observe?"

"That men fly to you like a bug to a zapper."

"Lovely. That's a lovely analogy. Yes, I'm a man-eater, Tom. You've pegged me completely and, what, you've come to this conclusion all from one stupid kiss? All because I made the gargantuan mistake of pressing my lips to yours?"

"Why do you keep talking about that? I never brought that up."

"Yes, but it's safe for me to assume that's where you're drawing all your reference from since the kiss has been our only real interaction with one another."

"You forget The Belle Jar party."

"So you flew to me like a bug to a zapper that night, did you? From what I remember, you called me a slut."

"I did *not* call you a slut, January! I said what you'd done was slutty."

"Ha! Same thing!"

"No, it's not, and I apologized for that already. I told you I didn't mean *any* of it." He exhaled loudly. "Besides! You weren't exactly innocent either! You played me that night! You dragged that confession out of me! God! I was such a sucker for it, too! I had no idea I'd fallen into your web until it was too late." He pointed at himself and said, "Bug!" Then pointed at me. "Zapper!"

I smiled smugly and crossed my arms, happily burying myself into my seat. "I don't know what you're talking about."

"Sure you don't, femme. Sure you don't."

"Excuse me?" I asked. "Listen, I just want to clear this up now, although I don't why because I don't owe you any kind of explanation, but if it'll make you stop being such a supreme ass with me, I'll fess up. I am *not* the kind of girl who kisses strange men. It was a one-time offense and you happened to be the victim, as you so seemingly are implying. I've only kissed two guys my *entire* life and you happened to be the second. I'm sorry. I'm sorry and it won't ever happen again. I swear on my life."

Tom narrowed his eyes briefly before fixing his expression to one of cool indifference. "Good."

The rest of the flight was met with uneasy silence.

Thomas

She's only kissed two guys? I almost couldn't believe her. She was so gosh damn beautiful, there was just no way that could be possible. I watched her. She bit at the side of her thumbnail as she argued with herself internally over whether or not her outburst was smart . It was. She put me in my place and I deserved it, not that I'd let *her* know that little fact nor would I let her know that her confession did a bit more than that. It made her even more intriguing, if that was possible. *Get a grip on yourself, Tom.*

When we exited the plane, January let me shoulder her carry-on without so much as a peep. I followed her up the Jetway out into the airport.

"Have you been to Ireland before?" I asked, my attempt at peace yet again.

She looked at me warily before deciding to answer. "The only places I've ever been are New Jersey where Grams lives and Austin. We'd visit New York City every now and then growing up, but that's about it. How about you?"

"I've traveled some," I answered vaguely.

We approached the customs counter and answered their questions.

"Where?" She pressed as we exited the main part of the airport and headed toward the luggage carousel. I held the door for her.

"Japan and all over Europe."

"Wow, when was this?" she asked, well aware as I was of this white flag moment.

"I was in a band before I joined Seven."

"No kidding. Who? Would I have heard of y'all?"

"I doubt it," I smirked as we came to a still before the empty revolving carousel. "We were called The Ivories."

Her mouth dropped open and she blinked lazily.
"What?" I asked.
"No, you weren't."
"Okay, I wasn't."
"Shut the hell up! You were not part of The Ivories."
"I was," I laughed.
She cleared her throat and her face burnt a bright red. I got it just then. Her face would always betray her. I tried not to do a little dance at that new development. "You guys were, uh," she swallowed, her face burning even brighter. She gently stamped her foot in frustration at the giveaway. "Amazing," she finished. "Really," she said, turning my way and looking me dead in the face. "I seriously loved the hell out of your music. I was so disappointed when I heard you disbanded."
She shocked me at that profession. "How did you even know about us?" I asked in disbelief.
A smile turned up at the corner of her mouth before she looked away then at the ground. "I made it my job to know good music, Tom. It's why I'm here...with you."
She made me smile but I turned away so she couldn't see.
The revolving carousel was now full of suitcases but we hadn't been paying attention.
"Let me know which one's yours," I gently commanded.
"All right," she conceded easily.
My duffel came into view and I reached to grab it, tossing it near our feet.
"That one," she said, pointing to another canvas duffel almost identical to mine but in a paler shade of green.
"Cool," I said.

An unguarded smile spread across her beautiful face and my hand slid slowly to my chest as a crackling feeling set deep within began to pop and shiver, another icy layer melting away.

January was like the freaking sun.

Chapter Four

Kiss With a Fist

Thomas

The label had a car waiting for us courtesy of a driver carrying one of those absurd signs with our names on it. Overkill. There was no one else around, but the guy held the sign up as we approached him like his job depended on it.

"Mister Eriksson?" A boy probably not much older than January dressed in a black suit asked in the thickest Irish brogue I'd ever heard.

"Yeah," I answered.

"Hi!" January exclaimed jauntily, reminding me she was definitely from Texas. She stuck her hand out, surprising the boy. "So nice to meet you!" she added.

The boy's face turned from surprised to exceedingly pleased as he drank her body in. He shook her hand vigorously. "A pleasure, miss. Here, let me," he said, dropping her hand and grabbing her bag.

I narrowly avoided a facepalm. Bug to a zapper.

"They're so nice here," she said to me under her breath as the boy led us to the car.

"Yeah, that's why he's being so nice," I said, but she didn't catch the sarcasm.

The boy-driver opened the back door to a black Mercedes. I didn't have the heart to tell January that this was the last decent piece of transportation she was going to see on our entire scouting adventure. She slid in and placed her hand on the back of the front seat ahead of her, her grip nervous. I slid in beside her as the driver placed our bags in the backseat.

"You okay?" I asked.

"Yeah," she said, her face contorting oddly as she forced a smile. *Terrible liar.*

The driver got in on the right side of the vehicle throwing me off for a moment.

"Uh, about how long to our hotel?" she asked the driver.

"I've been told to take you to Dublin HQ. Is that all right, miss?"

"Um, sure, of course. About how long?" she asked. I almost laughed as I turned my body slightly toward hers and took in her awkward body language.

"Right 'bout twenty minutes usually, Miss. But there's likely traffic on the M50 'bout this time 'a day.

I'd guess we'd arrive closer to half past, miss."

"Oh, okay," she said, wringing her hands. "Can I- Could I sit up there with you then?"

The boy looked at me briefly but his eyes lit up when they hit January's hopeful glance. "All yours, miss."

January floored me when she grabbed her bag and left me in the backseat on my own. I'm ashamed to say my mouth gaped. I was flabbergasted at the little minx.

"Thank you," she said, settling in beside him.

"No problems, miss." He smiled at her and I stifled the urge to knock his block off.

January rummaged through her purse as the boy pulled out of the airport and onto the M1. She pulled out a bag of ginger candies and offered me one.

I waved it away with one hand. "No, thank you," I said, still staring at her.

"Would you like one...I'm sorry, I never asked your name."

"Ailin, miss."

"January," she offered, smiling. "Would you like a piece of candy, Ailin?"

"Thank you, miss. I'd love one."

I sat stock-still when her hand reached over and handed *Ailin* a paper-wrapped ginger candy. My hand practically crushed the iPod I was holding when his fingers grazed hers. She turned her attention back to the sights around her but Ailin was having trouble paying attention to the road.

"Oy!" I said, startling Ailin back to the present. "Is this all you do for Seven?" I asked him through the rearview. His eyes met mine briefly and with a silent, cold, hard expression, I told him to let January go because, well, because I wanted him to.

"No, sir," he answered. "I'm a bit of a gofer for

them, really."

"Me too!" January exclaimed, turning back to Ailin.

"Really?" he asked excitedly before meeting my eyes again, swallowing hard. "Really?" he asked again but with less enthusiasm.

"Yeah," January answered. "At first, I only fetched coffee and that sort of crap, but with time, they gave me a few more responsibilities and were impressed. It's why I've been given the chance to become an apprentice of sorts with Tom here," she said, glancing back my way.

That and Jason thought it would be a fun game to throw us together, I thought.

"Anyway, don't give up," she said, patting his free hand, making *me* red in the face. *Calm down, Thomas!* "It'll pay off." She smiled warmly.

"Thank you," he said, slipping his hand from underneath hers. She frowned but didn't think more of it. Ailin's eyes met mine and I nodded.

We met all the necessary people at Seven, before Ailin drove us to the inn the label had set us up in. January sat up front again, inadvertently pissing me off.

"We should go out tonight," January said, surprising me.

"Seriously?" I asked her.

"Yeah," she continued, stepping around the front of the car to stand in front of me while Ailin unloaded our duffels. She looked up into my face and that's when I saw it. *Innocence*. She was going to kill me, I just knew it. "Ailin said a couple of his pals are going to Temple Bar tonight if we'd like to join them."

"Did he?" I asked her, eyeing Ailin as he hurriedly shuffled our bags inside without so much as a glance my way. "He included me in this invitation?" I asked, turning back her way.

She furrowed her brows as if what I'd asked was ludicrous. "Of course you're invited, Tom. I think it was mostly for you, anyway, and I was just included as a top off."

Sure. Zap. Zap.

"Yeah, Temple Bar is a blast," I admitted. "We can fish around for a few little bands as well, if you want."

"Oh, hell yeah! What a good idea."

I let January lead me into Anchor House, the inn the label had set us up in. It was charming, like most places in Dublin, and was just a short walk to Temple Bar, which would work out nicely for us. January was situated in the room directly across from mine and we each had a private bath, which was practically unheard of in little inns like these, but I was grateful because I wanted January's first night abroad to be a comfortable one. *Why do you even care*?

We agreed to meet at nine o'clock downstairs and would walk to Oliver St. John Gogarty's because *Ailin* wanted January to visit somewhere *authentic* for her first night. I kid you not, those were his exact words. He seemed pretty smug when all was said and done, but when I "accidentally" intercepted his hug goodbye to January, he seemed to get my message clearly, not that that would stop him, cheeky bastard. Didn't matter, I liked competition. I mean, not competition. I meant that - I just - you see - I didn't think it was a good idea for either one of us to get involved with people when we're supposed to be doing a job.

At six, I decided that I'd rather go run than eat because it'd been more than twenty-four hours since my last run and I was jonesing bad. I threw my garb on, a pair of Adidas track pants and a t-shirt, and went downstairs. Outside, I began to stretch against the railing.

The door opened, but I was too involved in my stuff to pay attention. That is, until I caught the whiff of January's perfume.

"Hey," she said, looking confused. Her eyes raked up and down my body. For some reason, this made me self-conscious. I'm assuming because she hadn't seen me in anything other than baggy jeans and heavy hoodies but I'm not sure why I gave a shit. "I didn't know you were a runner."

I took in her jogging outfit and thought the same. "Neither did I. You - that is, I meant to say, I didn't know *you* ran." *Smooth. Very smooth.*

"Mind if I join you?" she asked.

"Sure," I said, but amended, "but I don't talk when I run. That's when I listen to a lot of new music, actually."

"Same here," she said, holding up her iPod. This girl was all surprises.

Without another word, we began our jog. Since I'd been in Dublin before, for several weeks actually when I traveled with The Ivories (we'd had a crazy following here for some reason) and I was familiar with the strange cobblestone streets, I signaled for January to follow me. We jogged the River Liffey past Temple Bar for approximately two miles before crossing the bridge over the river and jogging Liffey the way back to Anchor House. The buildings were a pretty mix of old and new architecture. It fit Dublin so well.

A city of old, cherished tradition but the people weren't afraid of progress either. God, I loved Ireland. The last half-mile or so, I slowed down some to slow our heart rates. I was extremely impressed that January could keep up with me. It certainly explained the shape her legs were in. I'd yet to really see them, since it was dark at The Bowery, but their long, lean shapes definitely couldn't be hidden by the pair of jeans she'd been wearing the night we'd kissed. I'd noticed. I hated that I did but, all the same, I did.

I looked over at her transiently throughout the run. I found her to be one of the most beautiful women I'd ever met and that included Kelly, I was loath to admit. I couldn't deny it anymore, not when every male within a five-mile radius could sense her coming and would have jumped in front of a bus to make way for her. Every guy we passed, I wanted to punch in the gut for glancing her way. *God, I'm a mess.* For her, I was a slobbering mess. I hated it and loved it all at the same time.

She was a good five feet ten inches, possibly taller. She met my chin, which was practically unheard of. She had ridiculously long dark brown hair and blue eyes the color of the Atlantic. She was lean and beautiful and apparently talented according to Jason. He said she'd given up a full scholarship to Berkeley for piano. I was beginning to become enthralled with her and I absolutely hated it. I had to fight it. Had to.

When we reached Anchor House, we both leaned against the wrought-iron railing to catch our breath. We sat for a good five minutes before we were able to acknowledge each other.

"You're kind of a hoss," I admitted.

"So are you, actually," she said, wrapping the cord of her earbuds around her iPod. "Hear anything good?" she asked, gesturing to my own iPod.

"Maybe. I was partial to a couple of indies who were too good to want a label's interference, I think. There was one," I said, thinking, turning her way. "A band in Paris. Feel like crossing the channel?" I asked with a slight smile.

"Uh, um, of course," she said too cheerfully, even for January.

"*Okay,*" I said, skeptical.

"What's their name?" she asked, changing the subject.

"All The Pretty Girls," I admitted.

"Lame," she said, laughing.

"Yeah, but if all bands with terrible original names were turned down, we wouldn't have The Beatles or even Led Zeppelin."

"Yeah, Johnny and the Moondogs and the New Yardbirds would probably be playing pathetic hotel lounges right about now," she said, then snorted, shocking the shit out of me.

"You - how did you...?"

"How did *you*?" She rolled her eyes and jogged up the steps into the Anchor House and up to her room, leaving me with my jaw flush on the concrete below.

Zap.

After dozing off a bit after my run, I woke flustered to someone pounding on my door. I turned on my back, tired as hell from the time difference, and pulled my cell out. Eight-thirty. *Damn. Wait, I wasn't supposed to meet January until nine.* I dragged myself off the bed and threw the door open.

January stood at my feet, absolutely breathtaking and in one of the sexiest outfits I'd ever seen. The kicker? She was practically covered from head to toe, go figure.

"Is this okay?" she asked, frantic.

"What?" I asked, dazed from her sheer presence.

"Is this okay? For tonight? I have no idea what's appropriate anymore. People in the city don't dress like we do in Austin, Tom." I got a kick out of the fact that she associated me with Austin although I'd lived in New York my entire life. "So, I figured it was the same for Dublin." Her face bunched. "Help me?"

"This is fine," I said, not exactly telling the truth. The truth was, she made me want to rethink wanting to be alone. If she were my girl, Temple Bar could suck it and I'd just stay here, in this room with her, memorizing her face with my fingers and mouth.

"Are you sure?" she asked.

"Yes, I'm sure." I stepped inside and she followed, shutting the door behind her.

"Why aren't you ready?"

"Truthfully? You woke me up. If you hadn't stopped by, I would've probably missed meeting you downstairs."

"I'm sorry. Did you want to bail?" she asked. "I don't mind going alone."

Not if you paid me a million dollars, I thought, sinking another nail into my coffin.

"No, I'm cool now. I want to get out and listen to a few bands."

"All right, I'll meet you downstairs then."

I closed the door behind her and showered and dressed for Temple Bar quickly. I sat in front of the small mirror above my sink and wondered what the hell I was doing. I had no intention of looking for bands that night. I just wanted to stare at January. Oh, yeah, and make sure Ailin or anyone else for that matter, *didn't*. I took a long look at myself in the mirror. I was twenty-two years old and appeared thirty, but that wasn't because I physically looked thirty. It was because I wore my bitterness on my face like a second coat. I briefly thought for a moment if January could help me shed that coat but shrugged it off. I needed to remember that January would more than likely hurt the hell out of me and then I'd be an even bigger jerk than I already was and, to be honest, I was tired of being a jerk. It was wearing.

I took the stairs into the lobby below. The friendly desk clerk pointed outside. I opened the door and found January sitting on the stoop below me so I joined her.

"You ready?" I asked.

"Yup." She stood and wiped the dirt off her black skinny jeans. She carefully balanced herself down the steps on her ridiculous black heels.

"You're gonna break an ankle," I observed before grabbing her arm. A thick, syrupy heat spread through my hand and laced its way up into my chest, making another icy layer crack and spit in anger.

When she reached the walk, I let go like my hand had been at a hot stove. We walked in silence to Gogarty's, my hand repeatedly wanting to guide her by her lower back around potholes or stumps. I had to ring my arm in every time it reached out.

Gogarty's was packed even for a Friday from what I could remember, all tourists, but the unbelievable traditional music there was enough to wrangle even a few locals. The door swung open and we were hit with the fragrance of classic Irish cuisine, in other words, a bunch of meat and potatoes, and yeast but the music, the *music* that filled the pub was truly tangible. It rang in the air and swept over each expectant ear, swirling to the rooftop and guided back down. It was beautiful, incredibly beautiful.

Ailin saw us from across the bar and waved us over. We weaved our way through and he gestured to two empty seats beside him. January sat directly next to him and I next to her, but I got right back up.

"What'll you have?" I asked.

"Uh," she said, looking around, unsure.

My brows narrowed. "Do you drink, January?"

"Not really," she shrugged sheepishly. "Just get me whatever you're drinking."

I laughed. "I don't think you want what I'm having, sweetheart."

"Condescension. Nice touch."

"Fine," I said, lifting my hands in surrender. "I'll get you a pint of Guinness."

"Good," she said smugly, making me smile like a dumbass.

I leaned down into her ear. "Whatever you do, January, don't take a damn thing from these clowns. You hear me? We don't really know them." Her eyes were round in her head but she nodded. I sat back up and gestured to the others. "Pint, boys?" They shook their heads, their glasses over half full. Not half empty. Twenty-two years of Tie-Dye Tom couldn't be erased so swiftly after all.

I approached the bar and ordered two pints of Guinness instead of my usual McEwan's Scotch Ale. She would have been toe up from just the smell of it if I'd ordered her that. I gathered the pints and made my way back to January, setting the stout in front of her face and waited for her reaction. She smiled widely and picked up the pint. She hesitated, looking at me before bringing it to her lips.

"Drink up, baby girl."

"I *am*," she said, furrowing her eyebrows. "Stop ordering me around."

I sighed deeply.

She took a long, deep swig of the stout and her face contorted to impossible angles, making me laugh my ass off.

"What do you think?" I asked.

"I - I like it," she answered, her face still slightly knotted.

"I can tell."

She gave me a dirty look and I backed off, deciding to finally focus on the band playing that night.

They were just finishing up a lively tune when they shifted things a bit and started a deep, dark lament. January shot upright in her chair and grabbed my arm. “Molly Bán,” she whispered to me, never taking her hand from my bicep.

Molly Bán is a song of sad fates, a warning of sorts, meant for all young men.

Come all ye young fellows
That handle a gun
Beware of night rambling
By the setting of the sun
And beware of an accident
That happened of late
To young Molly Bán
And sad was her fate

She was going to her uncle’s
When a shower came on
She went under a green bush
The shower to shun
Her white apron wrapped around her
He took her for a swan
But a hush and a sigh
'Twas his own Molly Bán

He quickly ran to her
And found she was dead
And there on her bosom
Many salt-tears he shed
He ran home to his father
With his gun in his hand
Saying "Father, dear father

I have shot Molly Bán"

Her white apron wrapped around her
He took her for a swan
But a hush and a sigh
'Twas his own Molly Bán

He roamed near the place
Where his true love was slain
He wept bitter tears
But his cries were in vain
As he looked on the lake
A swan glided by
And the sun slowly sank
In the gray of sky

"How do you know it?" I whispered into her ear. Her body shivered. *Did I do that*?

She swallowed before answering. "My, uh, my Maimeó used to sing this to us when we were small." A small tear threatened from her glassy eye making me uneasy.

"What's a *Maw-mo*?" I asked, curious as hell.

"Maimeó is what we call my grandmother. She's born and bred Irish. Came to the United States, Jersey, in the sixties carrying my father."

"That explains the name MacLochlainn," I said, a slight grin tugging at my lips.

"Yeah, Americans assume I'm Scottish because of the whole 'Mac' thing but I'm one hundred percent Irish. My mother's family is Irish as well, but they came to the U.S. during the potato famine." That's when I realized that this must be like coming home for January.

"It also explains the red highlights," I blurted out without realizing. I almost slapped my hand over my mouth.

Her mouth began to form the question, but out of nowhere a man lifted me from my seat, saving me...possibly.

"Ah, it *is* you!" He exclaimed loudly for the whole pub to hear. He slapped me on the back, making me choke. "Right! Let's get pissed, ya' bastard!" He bellowed making everyone cheer.

"I'm sorry," I said, as he pushed me toward the bar, "do I know you?"

The guy had about ten seconds before I lost my cool.

"I'm sorry, friend! I know your band! The Ivories! Ah, right, see this here, I know your music. You were here, were ya' not, two years past?"

"I was. I can't believe you recognize me."

"Yeah, I didn't really like ya' much." How comforting, I thought as the ruddy, large Irishman eyed me like piece of meat. He smiled after a moment, making me nervous. My hand formed a fist in preparation. "It was my lady! Agh! Did she have it bad for ya'!" I tensed nervously. "What's the matter with ya'! Loosen up, man! What's ya' drink?"

The guy was all over the place. "What the hell!" I said, "I'll take a scotch, McEwan's."

"D'ya' hear this, boys? The Yank drinks *scotch*! 'Round here, them's fightin' words!" He said, pinching my shoulder hard. I tensed again. "I'm just joshin' ya', boy!" He laughed heartily and slapped me once more on the back.

I downed the scotch in one gulp, wincing as it burned its way down my throat.

"Another?" he asked.

"No, thanks. I've still got a pint at the table."

"That's not your table there, is it?"

"Uh, yeah, it is."

"No, it's not, mate! You're drinkin' with us tonight!"

I peered over my shoulder at January who had arched her back and leaned toward us, trying to listen in. When I caught her doing it, she righted herself, resting her chin in her hand on the table and pretended to be interested in Ailin's boring ass conversation.

"Is she with you?" The guy asked when he caught sight of January.

"Uh, yeah, that's January, but we're here with those guys," I said, though I don't know why I even mentioned it. This guy seemed infinitely more interesting than dumbass Ailin.

"They can come along then. Shane," the guy said, offering his hand.

"Tom," I answered, swiftly shaking his hand with enough grip to let him know I wasn't the type to take crap. This made him smile.

I tossed my head toward Shane's table, gesturing for January to follow and she stood. Ailin grabbed her wrist and for a split second I almost cocked back and hit the guy square in the jaw. She played it off with all the Southern charm I didn't know she possessed, picked up our pints and followed me over, making me feel smug and a little bit stupid all at the same time.

"Ailin's angry," she teased with a knowing smile.

"Is he?" I asked.

"Who's this guy?" she asked, nodding toward Shane.

"Apparently not a fan of The Ivories," I answered vaguely, making her brows furrow.

When we reached the table, Shane introduced us to his friends. "Tom, January," he said, smiling at her by way of introduction to which she beamed back, "this is Cillian, Douglas, Niam, Rowan, and," he beamed, "my lass, Siobhan." Together, these men were five of the most formidable men I'd ever come across in my entire life.

"A pleasure," January said, immediately sitting next to Siobhan, an instant friend, it seemed.

I nodded my greeting. I sat next to January and we got to know those strangers better than I would have ever thought.

"So, you're Irish, then," Shane inquired of January after an hour of drinking. We were all warm and friendly by this time but I mostly observed...January.

"Yes'sir," January slurred through a slight buzz. I was cutting her off.

"By what parts, miss?" Douglas asked.

"By Killarney."

"Shut your hole!" Cillian said, slamming his heavy hand on the table, making January jump then laugh. "That's me family's town! What'd ya' say your last name was?"

"I didn't, but it's MacLochlainn."

"Jesus, Mary, and Joseph! I know your Uncle Donovan!"

"Get out of town!" January exclaimed, eyes bright, and leaned Cillian's way.

"By the heavens, I knew you looked familiar. You've got your family's eyes, lass."

"Thank you," she said.

"'Twasn't meant as a compliment," he teased but she slapped his shoulder in retribution, making him laugh.

"My head's reelin'," Cillian said, looking on January. "Donovan MacLochlainn's niece in my very presence. By God, I've heard nothing but talk of your talent from here to kingdom come for years. The town's sick of it, but he carries on and on." He sat up and looked around. January grabbed my arm, making me wish I could glue her hand there, but I was too distracted to dwell because she appeared nervous. "James!" Cillian yelled across the room. "James! Have you your board tonight?" he asked one of the band members near the bar top.

"Aye!" James answered back.

"But I have a gift for you, James! A Yank! A bloody Yank who can play like an angel apparently." Cillian grabbed January's arm and hauled her to her feet, the look of surprise on her face made my heart race. I stood and grabbed her other arm.

"Come, darlin', none of us bite," he said, smiling.

"But - I haven't prepared anything. I haven't played Maimeó's songs in years!"

"It's like riding a bicycle, lass. 'Sides, you're Irish. It's in your blood!"

I was right in step beside January. "Do you want to leave?" I asked, worried.

She sighed but smiled. "The worst thing that can happen is that I forget and they boo me, right? Not so bad," she said, wringing her hands.

"Let's go," I said, taking her warm hand.

"No, no. I think I can do this. They don't call it liquid courage for nothing, right?"

I smiled.

January took the keyboards and began playing softly before winking my direction.

"An Irishman walks into a pub," she begins and the bar went silent. "The bartender asks him, 'What'll you have?'" Her Irish accent was spot on. "The man says, 'Give me three pints of Guinness, please.' The bartender brings him three pints and the man proceeds to alternately sip one, then the other, then the third until they're gone. He then orders three more.

"The bartender says, 'Sir, no need to order as many at a time. I'll keep an eye on it and when you get low, I'll bring you a fresh one.' The man replies, 'You don't understand. I have two brothers, one in Australia and one in the States. We made a vow to each other that every Saturday night we'd still drink together. So right now, me brothers have three Guinness stouts too, and we're drinking together.'

"The bartender thought this a wonderful tradition and every week the man came in and ordered three beers." January's playing and voice became more solemn, dramatic. "But one week, he ordered only two." The crowd oohed and ahhed. "He slowly drank them," she continued darkly, "and then ordered two more. The bartender looked at him sadly. 'Sir, I know your tradition, and, agh, I'd just like to say that I'm sorry for your loss.'

"The man looked on him strangely before it finally dawned on him. 'Oh, me brothers are fine - I just quit drinking.'"

The pub erupted in laughter as January played briskly through their whoops and hollers and when they'd quieted down, she stopped only to immediately start a heart-stopping rendition of Cooley's Reel. The pub kept beat on the wooden bar tops with their fists and the drummer joined in on the bodhrán.

I watched her. God, how I watched her. She was in her element, totally immersed in her playing and from the look on her face, probably didn't have any idea people were even listening. I knew that feeling. I reveled in that feeling when I was with The Ivories. She was amazing, breathtaking, actually, and that's when the realization hit me like a two-ton bomb. I was in the deepest of troubles.

Chapter Five

One Foot

January

When Cooley's Reel came to an end, I awoke from my piano-induced stupor to shouts and applause. I was rushed in that moment, not really even aware what people were so happy about. I searched the crowd for Thomas to see what he thought of my performance but came across Ailin's face first. He gave me a thumbs-up, so I smiled back. I continued my search but fell upon the wrong person's face again in Cillian.

"By heavens, lass! You are everything your uncle claimed you to be and more! I will never give him shite again!" He kissed the top of my head in drunken amazement before turning to talk to James, the Alba whistle player.

I searched the crowd again, almost frantic this time, for no real reason I could fathom other than I just wanted to see Tom's face. I smiled and shook hands politely, scanning the crowd until I caught his face in the back, standing by the tables we'd sat at earlier with Shane's friends.

He grinned softly at me, making my heart palpitate in my chest, my blood boil. No one and nothing had ever made me feel the way he did every time he looked upon my face. I felt the warmth of his gaze from the tips of my hair to the tips of my toes. My smile pulled on one side as I lifted my shoulders softly in a shrug. His grin got bigger and he shook his head at me. My nose crinkled and my smile began to match his, reaching both sides of my mouth. He gestured toward the door and we moved in unison until we met at the entrance. I pushed through the doors first and spilled out into the late night air.

Outside, I stood underneath the soft lamplight, reminding me of the scene from New York, the one where he thought I'd played him but, in truth, hadn't. I'd been just as surprised by his confession as he was. I just chose to let him think I wasn't. In hindsight, knowing how cynical he was, I shouldn't have done that. I was new to flirting and obviously so terrible at it he mistook my playfulness for cruelty. I was too embarrassed to correct the misunderstanding.

Tom approached me slowly and met me under the light on the stone walkway. He leaned over me so closely, my neck craned to see his face. His expression was one of confusion as he studied my own.

"What is it about you?" he asked me.

I gulped. "What do you mean?" I whispered, closing my eyes and swallowing again, my breaths becoming labored.

He lifted his hand and dragged the backs of his fingers across my jaw so lightly I barely felt them, but they made me feel dizzy all the same.

"How can you be this extraordinary, January MacLochlainn?" He leaned closer, a look of pure frustration and anger lit his eyes and pressed his lips. "And why couldn't I have met you before I realized I didn't want anyone...*ever*?"

"*What*?" I asked, astonished.

"Come on," he said, jerking me down the walk, but

I pulled back.

"Stop!"

"I have to walk you back to the inn," he said, with no feeling at all.

"No, stop. Just, stop for a second," I said, feeling like crying but not really sure why, I had no real reason to. I laid my hand over my pumping chest. "What did you mean by all that?"

"Nothing," he said, coldly staring right through me.

"Nothing," I said, searching his face for something more. "Nothing," I repeated.

"Nothing," he reiterated.

Oh God, what is this pain in my chest? "Let's go," I said, barreling past him.

"January!" We heard loudly, swinging both our attentions toward Gogarty's. *Cillian*. "Where're ya' goin', lass?"

"We've got an early start tomorrow," Tom said, answering for me, which angered me beyond belief, but I had some sort of strange indigestion and my chest hurt so I let him win that one.

Cillian stumbled down the steps toward us and grasped me in a fierce hug. "It was so nice to meet ya', January," he said into my ear, making the tears I'd been holding back fall. I'd been like that since I was young. Whenever I was struggling not to cry, the *second* someone touched me, the emotion would come spilling out of its own volition.

"It was a pleasure, Cillian," I said truthfully. I hugged him back to gain some time and eventually, God willing, some state of composure. Ironically, the same touch that made them spill is usually the same touch that helped me reel them back in. A strange dichotomy, I know.

Cillian pulled me away from him just as I gained control, but I averted my eyes to hide the rawness in them. "When you're in town next, lass, you look me up, right?"

"Zap," I heard Tom curiously mutter under his breath but didn't acknowledge it.

"Of course I will, Cillian."

"Just ya' ask any of the blokes in this bar, they'll point ya' my direction."

"Thank you, Cillian," I said, hugging him quickly before pulling away and waving goodbye as cheerfully as I could. Cillian watched us walk away for a moment before turning back to Gogarty's.

Tom and I walked in silence the entire distance to Anchor House and it was beyond deafening. When it came within sight, I practically sprinted down the walk and up the steps toward the door but, distracted by the pain in my chest, I fell and scraped my hands on the fourth step—completely humiliating me. The tears I'd gained control of thanks to Cillian now spilled in embarrassment, the pain in my chest pierced me tenfold. I felt Tom's breath catch before he reached for me.

"Don't touch me," I whimpered like a ten-year-old. "Please," I added, clearing my throat, "I'm fine."

I stood and carefully walked up the steps with my head held as high as I could get it, stiffening my back to the point it was almost painful. I felt Tom's presence behind me the entire time but that only served to magnify the pain in my chest exponentially. Without so much as a glance his direction, I stuck the key in my door with a tight "Goodnight, Tom" and steered my way inside. The bed beckoned to me and I found myself answering with a soft sob in its pillows.

I woke to a pounding head. No, not a pounding in my head, I realized, it was a pounding at my door. I got up, not bothering with my hair, though I knew it was a glorified mess. I swung the door open.

"Paybacks?" I asked a stoic Tom.

"Hardly. I've rented a car for our journey to London today. The ferry leaves at eight forty-five. Meet me downstairs in fifteen." And with that, he turned and walked back downstairs.

I saluted his back. "Good morning, January. Nice to see you. Have a nice sleep, did you?" I closed the door. "Jerk."

Fifteen minutes doesn't mean jack crap to me in the mornings. It takes me that long to pee. Seriously. I'm like a snail in the mornings. I supposed I'd have to get used to things like that on the road. I sighed loudly and ran to the bathroom, turning on the shower. I glanced in the mirror and noticed I still had my clothes on from the night before. That probably made Tom cluck his tongue at me. He was such a "judger." *God!* I stripped and landed in the shower, washing my hair and shaving my legs in less than five minutes. Another two minutes for my teeth. Three minutes later, I was stuffing everything into my duffel after dressing in a thermal, one of my The Belle Jar t-shirts, jeans, and black boots.

Hair wet, no makeup, I slammed my hotel door home, ran down the stairs, and skidded to a halt in front of Tom checking us out at the front desk.

"Good morning!" The clerk greeted me.

"Good morning!" I answered cheerfully back. "So nice to see a friendly face this early in the morning!" I added, staring straight at Tom with the largest smirk on my lips.

I hauled ass past his glare and down the stairs, arriving at what I assumed was our rental since it was just across the street and in the back laid Tom's duffel. *Copycat*. I tossed mine beside his and shut the hatch to the impossibly tiny rental. *God, I'm going to have to share this with him! There's barely enough room for one, let alone his gigantic ass*! I tossed my purse/hobo-bag/lifeline on the hood of the car and rummaged through my bag for my makeup. Leaning over and peering into the window, I applied a little rouge, mascara, and lip gloss. Just enough for myself to appear somewhat human then turned my head over and brushed my long hair, trying so hard to keep the tangles out of its impractical length. I flipped it back over and detangled from there. I threw my brush back into my bag and ran my fingers through it, trying to get it to dry as quickly as possible. I was done.

I looked at the tiny car and the potential proximity and thought twice. I reached back into my bag and spritzed a tiny bit of perfume, enough to tickle the nose but not enough to suffocate you in the car, then applied a bit of color to my lips and a thin layer of liner to my eyes. I shook my hair out and checked my reflection. *Almost.* I reached back in my bag and grabbed a small rubber band as well as a black chopstick. I loosely braided a French braid waterfall at the top and side of my head, leaving a few tendrils loose, tied it off, then wrapped the entire thing and all the loose hair into an unkempt bun at the side of my nape opposite my braid, stabbing it together with the chopstick. The effect was a sweeping look and it was beautiful. It always got me compliments. Ahem. Always. *Good enough.* Good enough? Good enough for whom, January? *Oh, shut up!*

Tom exited Anchor House at the precise moment I turned around. He stopped dead, dropped whatever papers he was holding and his keys but the kicker was when he bent to retrieve them, his eyes wouldn't leave mine, that's when I knew I had him. His hands rummaged the concrete below him haphazardly, making him flustered when they turned up empty. Eventually he pulled away to find what he'd dropped. *Ha! I'll take that compliment, thank you very much, Thomas Eriksson.*

"Let's go," he said, stepping in front of me.

I turned around and started to open the door. Tom's hand reached out at my ear and kept me from opening it, heating me up from the inside at his proximity.

"No," he said, making me turn around. His nose was inches from mine. He smelled like soap, aftershave and wintergreen Altoids.

I breathed deeply. My eyes felt heavy. "No?"

"This is the driver's side, remember?" he said, waking me from my trance.

"Oh," I said sheepishly. "Sorry."

I slipped out from underneath his arm and rounded the car to the passenger side. I opened the door, sat, and put on my seatbelt. I stared out the window, chewing my thumbnail and cursing myself for tying up my hair. The red blush I felt coming hit me with a vengeance and there was nowhere to hide. *Stupid blood.*

Thomas

Good God, January was a *beautiful* woman. When she came down the stairs, all fresh, no makeup, hair damp and down her back, I thought I was going to keel over at how feminine and natural she looked, but when I came outside and saw that she'd braided her hair like she was ready for a red carpet event in the five minutes I'd been away from her, I was definitely floored. Or, "concreted" depending how you looked at it.

I blundered around like an idiot at my own feet

staring at her incredible face. I'd given her fifteen minutes—not actually thinking she'd only take the fifteen minutes. Weren't women supposed to take twice as long as the time limit given them? She was supposed to take longer, and then I was supposed to give her shit for it. After all that, she was supposed to put me in my place. That's how it was supposed to work. She made me feel like an idiot in so many ways. Particularly in this moment because we were going to be hella early and it was all because I put a ridiculous time limit on this gorgeous girl just because I felt like being an ass. And I was.

I got in the car and belted myself in. I glanced January's direction and noticed her neck was a flaming red. All I could do was smile like an imbecile at that knowledge. She was flushed and I'd deciphered that she only became beet red for one of two reasons. One, she was flustered because she was embarrassed or, two, she was flustered because she was attracted to whomever she was talking to. My smug ass was sure this flush was the latter because, well, *I* was attracted to her in the previous moment, but that didn't make me feel as pissed off as I'd been when it had happened before. No, it made me excited and hopeful, therefore making me pissed off at myself for not being pissed off. *I'm an idiot.*

I started the car and put it in drive before jetting off onto the cobblestone road and taking a left on Beresford. We were at the port in less than fifteen minutes. Luckily, there were cars lined up to board the ferry, which essentially looked like an overgrown speedboat, if I was being honest. That made me slightly nervous, but apparently the Dublin Swift would take us to Holyhead in North Wales in less than two hours and that would work out perfectly for time as we could be in London by five in the evening, leaving us just enough time to rest and go out that night. There were three bands the label wanted us to look at.

"Couple of things," I said, breaking the silence. January jumped. I cleared my throat. "Sorry. Anyway, um, we should be in London by this evening. There're three bands there Seven wants us to look at and I know of two for sure that I have been wanting to see since meeting them both in New York when I was with The Ivories."

She turned her alluring head my direction and I bit my lip to keep myself from rushing across the tiny space and kissing off her face. "Five bands in one night!"

"Yeah, I know it's the pits, but they don't like paying our bills if it doesn't prove worth it, catch me? This is a hard job, January. It doesn't pay shit. You get no job assurance, no perks, no sleep. When you do get to sleep, it's in some shady places sometimes, but it's worth it for most of us because we get paid to listen to music. You think you can hang?"

She furrowed her brows at me. "Anything you dish my way, I can take. Trust me. I'm a big girl."

Good thing the car was in drive or I would have lifted her into my lap at that last comment. "I'm sure you can," I said, not able to help myself.

"What?" she said, whipping her head back around.

"Nothing, I mean, we don't have to stay for all the songs in their sets, you know. We can get a feel for them and if we don't like it, we can move on."

"Oh, okay, that's cool."

As the line to board our car inched closer to the ship, I noticed January's hand twisting in circles. She kept worrying her lip and pinching her brows. Her breathing got deeper and she actually started to worry me.

"You okay?" I asked, concerned.

"What?" she asked, turning my way again, her lips pursed.

"You okay?" I said, laughing. "You look ready to jump ship and we haven't boarded yet. You afraid to sail?"

"Uh, something like that," she said, fretting at her hands.

"It's okay. I'm not going to lie to you, it's a bit of a rocky ride but it's completely safe." A small squeak sounded from her side of the car. "January?" I asked.

But she couldn't answer me because we were asked to follow the line ahead of us to board. I obeyed the guy's gesture up the ramp and parked behind the long line of cars. January and I both got out and after I locked the car doors, we headed up the steel grate stairs into an elaborate lobby, similar to something you'd see on a cruise ship but much smaller in size.

I pointed to a lounge area where a few people were already mingling about and we sat. January plopped her purse on her lap and started sifting through its contents, lazily at first but grew more frantic as time passed.

"January?" I asked but she didn't answer. "January," I said a bit louder but still no response. "January!" I practically yelled.

She looked up at me and her eyes were wide and distraught. "My medicine," she said as if I'd understand.

"Your medicine," I repeated.

"Yes, my medicine. I - I need it and it's not here. I must have packed it in the duffel." She stood up, right as the captain was making his announcement we were leaving port.

"You can't go down there, January. All the doors to the cars will be locked. It's too dangerous."

She seemed to become overwrought at that news and I felt like my heart was going to pound out of my chest. *Oh my God, what if these pills are a matter of life and death.*

"Come on," I said, grabbing her hand in mine. Instead of the usual warmth I'd felt before, they were ice cold. As we walked, I couldn't stop myself from warming them between my own. "What," I said, before taking a deep breath, bracing myself for news she had some crazy heart condition or something. "What are the pills for?" I tried to ask breezily.

"Motion sickness," she said, shocking me. The adrenaline I'd felt preparing myself for bad news turned to anger.

"What!" I asked too loudly.

"I didn't want to tell you," she said, fidgeting near the door. "Excuse me," she asked a ship employee, "but I've left something in our car. Is it possible to retrieve it?"

The employee, a young man, probably my age, frowned at her, looking like it broke his heart that he couldn't help this damsel in distress. *Zap*. I wanted to punch him. "I'm sorry, miss, but once the ship leaves dock, these doors go on automatic locks."

"Oh, okay," January said, deflated. The man walked away but not without glancing back once more.

"January."

"Hmm?" she asked, distracted.

"You have motion sickness. Like, when you sail?"

"Uh, not exactly."

"Tell me then."

"Um, I get motion sickness on everything. Car, train, boat, plane. You name it, I get sick...and not just a little sick either."

"January MacLochlainn," I said, scrubbing the back of my neck in frustration. "How the hell did you think you were going to do this job, huh? It's nothing *but* traveling."

"Listen, this isn't a handicap, okay? I can travel, I just need meds to do it." Her eyes went wide and she placed her hand over her mouth. "It's happening," she said as the boat tipped and weaved in the water, ready to sail.

"Oh no, it's not," I said, grabbing her hand and heading to the shops on the ship. "God, I should have known when you offered that ridiculous ginger candy that only my grandmother would eat."

"Please don't mention food," she whined.

I could only sigh my frustration.

Truthfully? I was more upset that she was in any kind of pain. For some reason, the idea of this girl in agony made my stomach twist. In the nearest shop, I ducked inside and got a lemon-lime carbonated drink that looked like Sprite and a few boxes of seasick meds. I slid Seven's credit card because I'd forgotten my own back in the car. I didn't want to think about how I was going to explain these weird charges to Jason. He could just suck it, January was ill.

"Come on," I said to a very green looking January. She leaned on me, which let me know just how ill she was. I knew her well enough to know she wouldn't have done it unless things were dire. She'd wanted me to think she hated me. I dragged her to a window seat and sat her down. I tore off the cap to the soft drink as quickly as possible and handed it to her.

"Start sipping," I said. She took it and brought her trembling hands to her mouth.

I ripped open the box of what I thought looked the most promising, relief-wise, in the shop and handed her the two pills. She downed them quickly and I sat beside her, reading the label to the other box to make sure I could mix the medicines if the other didn't work. I picked up her bag and dug out her ridiculously ginormous bag of ginger remedy/old lady candy and unwrapped a piece.

"Take it," I said, handing it to her.

She shifted her body around so she wouldn't be facing the ocean. I dragged her closer to me and made her lean her head on my shoulder. I rubbed up and down her arm until she seemed to feel better, her breathing becoming steady again.

"Thank you," she said to the air in front of us.

"Of course," I said. *I hate seeing you hurt. I'm sorry for hurting you last night. The look on your face speared my icy heart. I wish I could take it all back.* But like a coward, I didn't say any of it. I couldn't bring myself to say the words.

She sat up, leaving my side bereft of her warmth. "Do you know why you're with me here, January?"

"Because I'm being punished by God?"

"You're being groomed," I told her, ignoring her jab.

"Pass me that banana, will ya'?" she teased.

"Good to see you're feeling better. It was touch and go there for a while," I joshed back.

She smirked. "So you're grooming me."

"For my job," I said.

Her brows creased. "Why? Are you leaving Seven?"

"No, I'm being considered for a position on the upper floor. Management, baby," I said, not realizing I'd said baby until it was too late. Her eyes popped wide for a moment. I cleared my throat. "Management. Mom would be so proud."

"No shit. When?"

"It's not when it's *if.* Jonah and I are both vying for the same position. This little international excursion is a test, a competition."

January thought for moment before the most mischievous look on her face crossed her features. "We'll beat 'em."

She made my heart pound. "We will?" I shifted my feet around a bit.

She rolled her eyes. "I know your ear for music and I know his. We're going to beat him."

We're *going to beat him*, she'd said. "If you say so," I said, turning my head toward the water but feeling an ache in my chest the likes I'd never felt before. I barely stopped my hand from grabbing at my heart.

January fell asleep on my chest half an hour into our journey and I hated how much I loved looking at her as she slept.

January

Thomas thought I'd fallen asleep on his chest. I knew this because after I'd taken the liberty of using his chest as a pillow and a few minutes had passed in silence, I'd opened my mouth to tell him what an incredible ass I thought he was but was struck mute when he tentatively began to rub my arm. I fought the goose bumps threatening to betray me and paid great attention to the movement of his hand.

At first, he used only the tip of his index finger, experimenting with a mere graze here and there. I guessed when he felt like I was properly asleep because I felt the weight of all his fingertips explore the surface of my arm, but he always remained above the elbow, still testing the waters it seemed. He traced the contours of my arm over and over almost driving me insane but just when I was about to shiver uncontrollably, he placed his entire warm palm on my arm and guided it down to my wrist then back up.

It was the sexiest thing I'd ever experienced and it was only my bleeping arm. He stopped and I wanted to cry out for him to continue, but he surprised me when I felt his warm palm cross my nape and throat. He guided his hand up to the back of my neck and back down to my shoulders. My breathing got deeper and I fought to regulate it, swallowing as silently as possible so not to scare him off.

"So soft," he barely breathed, making me melt at this unseen side of him.

His hand followed my arm down again until he reached my hand. He picked it up and rubbed his thumb over the back of my hand before threading his fingers through my own, holding them there. I wanted so badly to squeeze his grip, to let him know I knew and that it was okay, but couldn't bring myself to ruin the amazing moment. The moment I discovered Thomas Eriksson was nothing but a fake. His river ran much deeper than I imagined, and I knew this from his careful and remarkably affectionate touch. He was a master at the game of pretend, but I knew all his secrets in this tiny slip of his guard and I planned on disarming him completely...by Paris. *Careful, Thomas.* I thought. *I've got your number.*

That's when my eyes closed in sincerity. I'd never fallen asleep so easily and I had Tom to thank for that.

***

"You seem to sleep on me very easily," Tom said, waking me.

I turned over in his lap and looked up into his face, smiling like I knew something he didn't. "Good morning?" I asked.

"Yes, but it's close to eleven now. We're docking soon. Now, actually. We should be able to get to our car within the next fifteen minutes."

I sat up and stretched, still smiling. He'd let me sleep on him the entire ferry ride.

"What?" he asked, suspicious.

"Nothing," I said, checking my stupid grin.

People were lining up at the doors to access their cars and we followed suit. Inching closer and closer as the *Dublin Swift*'s employees guided everyone to their vehicles. We weren't allowed to start our cars until they'd opened the lift to the dock so we sat in absolute silence, waiting.

"How long have you played the piano?" Tom asked, drumming his fingers on the wheel of the car.

"Since I was four...so, about fifteen years. My grandmother taught me at first when she lived in Austin, before she relocated back to Jersey."

"Is that where you learned Cooley's Reel?"

"Yeah, I know a bunch of silly Irish tunes like that."

"You're talented," he said, making me blush to my toes.

"Thank you, but you don't have to lie," I teased.

"I'm not," he bit out, very serious and startling me. "I'm not," he repeated, softer. "You're truly gifted, January."

"Th-thank you," I said, staring at him in astonishment. "So are you."

He scoffed at that. "No, I'm not."

"Bullshit," I said.

"Excuse me?"

"Bull. Shit. You are talented. You forget, I knew your band before I knew you. I know who wrote all your songs. It was your name on almost every track."

"Yeah and a fat lot of good that got me."

"It may not have gotten you signed, but that's the

luck of the draw in my opinion. You and I both know there are a million bands out there that didn't make it but are just as, if not more, talented than those who have. Maybe that's why you're here, in this car with me, waiting to see five bands in London. You know what talent really is, and you can help push it to the front of the queue with Seven."

He dragged the side of this thumb across the top of the steering wheel and I accepted that as a form of acknowledgement.

"Besides I'm kind of glad you didn't make it."

"Nice, January."

"No, really. Listen, if you had made it, I'd have never..." *kissed you*, "met you and wouldn't have gotten the ultimate lesson in scouting under such *awesome* tutelage. Call me selfish, but I'm happy to be sitting here with you."

He looked at me and shook his head, a tiny grin gracing his lips. *Bingo*.

"I think you're incredibly suited for this job, Tom. It may not be what you had imagined yourself doing, but fate has a way of stepping in and guiding you the direction you need to go even when you yourself had no intention of creating that path." I sighed deeply.

A chorus of engines started as the lift to the ferry opened up and Holyhead's blue sky greeted us.

"We need to feed you," he said out loud, not really talking to me.

"Thanks, I'll just get my bib and rubber-coated spoon then."

"Shut up," he said, laughing and surprising me.

"I just meant that if we're going to be on the road for a while and what with your little issue, you probably need to eat something to keep you from feeling ill."

"Oh, thank you," I said, genuinely touched that he

even thought past the minute with me.

"Yeah, don't mention it."

Our little rental putted down and out into the fresh sea air.

"Pass this way with a pure heart," I said, reading an inscription on a bit of concrete just off the port.

"Holyhead's motto."

"Very pretty."

Tom grunted his reply. I suppose it was better than nothing.

"I know of a fish and chips shop just off Cambria in the city proper. Cherry found it when The Ivories were here a few years back."

"Sure," I said. "Cherry, from The Ivories Cherry?"

"Yeah."

"Oh my God, she is so freaking cool. I love the crap out of her."

"She is cool, my Cherry Bomb. She's a sister to me."

"Tell me about your friends." I knew this was a subject he wouldn't shy away from. It was the one topic that made Tom's eyes light up like the Fourth of July.

"They're my family. You probably know all about The Ivories, but there're a few more of them who don't take a stage at all but are so extraordinary they should.

"For instance, besides Cherry, Callum and Harper are my best friends. I hang or *hung,* before I moved to Austin, with them almost every other day. January," he said, meeting my eyes for a moment before moving them back to the road, "they are so freaking amazing. Both of them grew up in the foster system and were kicked out at eighteen with nothing but the shirts on their backs. They met, worked themselves up from nothing and are becoming some of the most accomplished people I've ever met in my entire life!

And they never asked for anything. They became extraordinary all on their own." He shook his head and took a deep breath. "I miss them so much," he said, his neck and face heating up at their memory. He was fighting with emotion so badly it was affecting his heart, I could tell.

"I want to meet them," I said, trying to keep him there with me, to keep him from reverting back to his closed-off normal self.

"So do I," he said, shocking me mute. "They'd love you."

"Thank you," I barely whispered as we pulled up to the chip shop.

We walked into the tiny little shop and bought an order of fish and chips to share. Turns out, we both liked vinegar and salt on our chips so I lucked out there. With drinks in hand, Tom and I sauntered across the street and set our food on the wall between us and a very beautiful cemetery.

"What's with your name, January?" he asked.

"Oh," I laughed, rolling my eyes, "my parents."

"Oh, really, that's fascinating. Your parents named you, did they? What a conversationalist!"

"Shut up, rude ass. My parents named each of us after the months of the year."

"Starting with you, then."

"Yes, and it goes all the way down to October. My mom lost her eleventh and couldn't have them anymore. So, we're stuck at ten kids." I smiled.

"Ten kids! My God, that is - that is a lot of kids."

"Yeah, but you've never had so much fun as you've had with my family. They are the craziest, funniest, most amazing people in this world. The way you feel about your friends is the way I feel about my family."

"Then you must love them very much," he said softly, eyes trained on a few grave markers.

"I do. My sister July is my best friend. She is so rockin' cool, Tom. She's got this crazy long, jet-black hair and is, like, six feet tall. She's bigger than life!" I smiled at a memory of her. "All of us are pretty tall. I'm the shortest actually."

"You're the *shortest*?" he asked in disbelief, his eyes roaming down then up my body and heating me up from the inside without so much as a graze of his hand.

"Yes." I cleared my throat.

"I imagine your family must be an imposing force."

"That they are, but not because of their height. We're just big and loud and lots of fun. I miss them already."

"It'll be alright," he offered. "You're going to have a lot of fun at this job, trust me."

I eyed him carefully, taking in his tall frame, stopping on the hand that rubbed my arm not two hours before. *I have a feeling you're right, Thomas Eriksson.*

"So you know how lucky I am in my heritage but what about you? Where does Eriksson come from?"

"My mom is Swedish and my pop is American but from German descent."

"Ah, that explains the light features," I said, popping another chip in my mouth and contorting my face from the vinegar.

"Yeah, blond hair, blue eyes. Boring."

"Oh, I wouldn't say boring," I said, my face and neck heating to an impossible color. *Irritating problem!*

Tom's tongued his upper teeth as he avoided a laugh and that proceeded to drive me up the bloody wall.

"Sorry," I said, hiding my face behind my hands.

"Don't," he said, pulling at one of my wrists. "It's nice, January."

Nice? Nice? What does that mean*?*

"Come on," he said, crumpling the coned newspaper that carried our chips and tossing it in the nearest bin. "We've got quite a trek ahead of us."

Chapter Six
El Scorcho

January

Our tiny car proved advantageous for "Operation Disarm Tom." He kept glancing my way, his arm bumping mine, his shoulder grazing mine, his fingers brushing mine. Problem? Uh, it was slightly backfiring! I kept fantasizing he'd veer off the road and onto the shoulder and kiss the tar out of me.

"Tom," I said, gulping down the tension permeating throughout the car.

"Mmm, hmm," he said, his knuckles white.

"Can we pull over?"

"Why?" he asked, his eyes wide. "Feeling sick?"

I was sick—just not from motion sickness. "Uh, yeah."

Tom pulled over and I struggled with my belt, bolting from the car. I discovered we were on top of the most gorgeous rolling hill, its green sweeping layers screamed beautiful things as the wind swooped around the feet and back to the heads of

each mounded hill.
Wales.

It was one of the most breathtaking countrysides I'd ever had the pleasure of witnessing. A quaint little town was nestled at the bed of the hill below and it looked like what I'd envisioned a village two hundred years ago would look like, like time had stood still. The only things that gave away progress were the little cars winding the charming streets.

I was breathing hard from the proximity of Tom and the overwhelming view below me. Tom came and stood beside me, brushing a few strands that had strayed from my loose braid from my shoulder.

"You okay?"

I looked up at him. "Um, yeah. Much better. Thank you for pulling over."

"Of course," he said, moving to see the view I'd just admired. "Wow," he exclaimed, "why do I feel the need to abandon my life as I know it and start a new one here?"

I laughed. "Because you're sane? This is an incredible place. Look at that view." I held my hands out in front of me.

"Extraordinary," he said, but when I looked up to agree with him, his eyes weren't on the world around us, they were trained on me. My neck and face heated, but I didn't find myself embarrassed.

"What?" I asked.

"Nothing, we should, uh, get on the road," he said, walking back to the rental.

"Alright." I sighed. "Wait," I said stopping him short by grabbing his arm. "You've got something on the back of your hoodie." I dusted away imaginary nothings from his back, enjoying the unbelievably amazing muscles beneath his hoodie.

"Get it?" he asked.

"Oh, I got it." I smiled at myself before settling in and buckling myself back in.

***

London was five hours away and I took the opportunity to get to know Tom a little better, asking him all his favorites. Favorite color, food, song, band. I packed as much as I possibly could in those five hours and by the end of it, I felt I knew Thomas Eriksson better than anyone possibly could in five hours with the impossible Thomas Eriksson.

Truth be told, I was surprised he'd opened up at all—let alone the amount he'd shared. The crazy part was for every question he answered, he expected me to answer the same, like he wanted to know as much about me as I wanted to know about him.

But an hour from London, the most unfortunate thing happened...Well, unfortunate yet at the same time *very fortunate*. You'll see.

"Is Jonah going to be there?" I asked, fiddling with the stations. "At the shows tonight?"

"Yeah, it's definitely a competition. He'll be wherever we'll be, I think."

"Tell me about the bands. Who are they? How long have they been playing? Any past affiliations? Spill," I said.

"Well, the first band's been signed before to an independent label called Red Flag. Familiar?"

"Yeah, they've got Hope Nesting and Katie Butler. They've got the right idea, but they're just starting out. Why'd they leave Red Flag?"

"Differences in opinion. Probably in the studio. The problem I see is that they're good, but not good enough for Seven. I mean, I can see that they might have potential but..."

"But why invest when I can name ten bands off the top of my head that need no conditioning? Who are ready to market immediately with slight finessing?"

"Exactly."

"What's their name?"

"The Mark."

"Know 'em," I said.

"*Really?*" He asked, obviously surprised. "And what's your opinion?"

"Honestly? They're a Caged ripoff, and I hate to say it but Caged is on the down and out. Kaput."

"Exactly!" He nearly yelled, making me jump. I was so unused to him raising his decibel level above "I'm cool," that if I'd been standing, I'd have fallen over, like one of those ridiculous stunned goats. "Exactly," he repeated but softer.

"All right," I said, feeling bolstered by his almost-praise. "What about the rest?"

"Okay, uh, trying to remember." He drummed his talented fingers on the steering wheel. "Oh, yeah, ever heard of London-based..."

The car spit and sputtered and completely broke down. Tom pulled it over, removing the keys from the ignition.

I expected him to curse, lose his temper, yell, something, but he didn't. "Well, that sucks," he simply said. He was as calm as I'd ever seen him and that impressed me.

"What are we going to do?" I asked. It was October. The sun was destined to set in another hour. In fact, the sky was a deep pink and orange, the beautiful precursor to night.

"We find a phone," he said, getting out. "Knew I should have gotten a cell in Ireland. Oh well. All right," he said, peering behind us. "There's nothing behind us for miles. We march onward."

I followed Tom for a few yards, wishing to all that was holy I'd just put on my thicker coat. I hadn't expected it to get so flipping cold so fast but England winters, it seemed, were much harsher than I was accustomed to, being born and bred in Texas. My fingers were freezing and my nose felt like it was on fire. I was willing to bet that wasn't a good sign.

As we walked side by side, Tom didn't say a word, too deep in thought, but he was definitely paying attention because out of nowhere, he slid off his big leather jacket and wrapped it around my torso, squeezing it around me.

"I can't take your coat, Tom."

"You can and you will," he said. "I've got this thick hoodie."

Since asking for permission was out, I decided to act first, apologize later. I huddled up next to him and wrapped my arms around his waist. I closed my eyes briefly, waiting for the rejection I was sure would come, but he only wrapped himself around me as well and we walked nestled together toward the glowing lights of a petrol station.

It was small, only two pumps, but they had a store inside and we were both excited about that because we hauled ass a few feet from the entrance. When the door slid open, warm air engulfed us.

"Thank God," I said, making Tom laugh.

"Anyone home?" Tom called out to the empty store, pulling away from our embrace. I'm not gonna lie, I felt a little devastated that our hug was over, but we had a job to do and we needed a phone.

I peeked around doors, even knocked on the restroom stalls, but no one seemed to be around.

"That's odd," Tom said circling around. "There's no payphone. Besides that, I've got no money but American."

I looked around and behind the register and noticed the phone was setting on a small area behind that. "Should we just use it anyway? What time is that first show?"

"Ten. I think if we can just get the rental company to come replace the car, we'd be able to make it. We're only an hour outside London."

"All right," I agreed. I leaned over the register and picked up the phone just as the store employee came rounding a bend we hadn't seen.

"Oy! What ya' doin'!"

"Nothing!" I said. "We just needed to borrow your phone. We're stranded about a mile that way." I pointed down the road but it did no good.

"Stay right there!" He yelled to Tom as he grabbed my wrist hard.

"Sir! Please! You don't understand, we just needed to borrow your phone," I said.

Tom came at my side, huge and intimidating and the guy dropped my wrist. "We meant no harm," he said, but the guy had already grabbed the phone from me and dialed the police.

"Yes, I've two thieves at...Yes, that's it. That's it." He hung up. "Stay put, you two! " We stood there, determined to clear up the misunderstanding. Tom crossed his arms over his chest. I could tell he was holding back. The veins in his arm pulsated and his neck strained with the tension. "Just stay put!" The novice detective said.

"We're here, aren't we?" Tom asked, losing patience. "If we were truly thieves, why would we be standing here? Are you purposely being obtuse?"

The man said nothing, just shifted from foot to foot waiting for his "rescuers."

"Should we just leave?" I asked.

"Nah, they'll just put out a search for us and we did nothing wrong, why should we run? Plus, our getaway car is done."

"Good point."

Ten minutes later, two policemen walked through the door and braced themselves at the entrance.

"Henry," one of the coppers said, but it sounded more like, 'Enry.

"I caught these two Yanks stealin'."

"Oh my God!" I said, throwing my hands into the air. "For the last time, we were not stealing! When you came in, I was holding the phone!"

"Just a moment, miss," Officer Two said. "Go on, Henry. Tell us what happened."

"I come 'round 'ere," he said, pointing to the impossible corner he emerged from, " an' this one was attemptin' the register!"

Tom started to laugh. "Haven't you any cameras? You can see for yourself. We were not stealing."

"All right," the first cop said, "what were ya' doin' 'hind there anyhow?"

"She told you correctly," Tom explained. "Our car stalled a mile or so down the interstate there and we were looking for a phone. We came in, looked around for someone to ask since there's no payphone and no one was here. We have to be in London by ten tonight and needed to call the rental company. That's when we saw a phone just behind the counter. Granted, it wasn't the smartest idea we'd ever had, but it's the truth nonetheless. Here," he said, pulling out the rental agreement. "You can check down the road, there should be a small car parked on the shoulder. I brought the contract to answer any questions they'd have."

"Sounds reasonable," Officer One said. "David, run down an' see this car."

"Right."

Officer Two, David, left the store and left the parking lot to spy it out.

"You're thieves," the employee said, but he was losing steam because his once defiant chin now sagged near his chest.

"Are not," I said.

"Are too," he spit back.

"Are not!" I said.

"January," Tom said, looking at me like I was the biggest idiot, shrugging his shoulders in question.

I shrank into myself at the immaturity of it, but I couldn't help it! The guy was getting on my last nerve!

Officer David came waltzing back in, a pair of handcuffs dangling from his hand. "None of it, chap. There's no car there."

My mouth dropped to my own chest this time. "Not possible!" I exclaimed.

Tom, cool as a cucumber, said, "Then I'd like to report a stolen vehicle."

"Come then," Officer One said, gesturing to Officer David. "You too, miss. You're both comin' with me."

All I could do was watch Tom, desperation seeping from every pore I owned. "Tom?"

"Just do as they ask, January. We'll get this all straightened out."

"Oh God! My mother is going to kill me. She always dreamed of my first arrest but theft isn't exactly the charge she'd imagined."

"Stop being so dramatic. This is a simple misunderstanding." Tom thought for a moment. "What kind of charge would she have preferred?"

"Oh, I don't know. Probably something like unlawful protesting or resisting arrest?"

"You can still accomplish resisting arrest."

"Awfully odd for thieves, ain't they?" Officer One asked David.

"Yanks are an unusual lot, they are," David responded.

Officer One handcuffed me and David cuffed Tom.

Agh! Our duffels! "Tom! All our stuff!"

"Don't worry about it. Jason will take care of us."

They stuck us in the back of their police car and I was forced to lean a bit into Tom at the awkwardness of our positions. "You're just too big," I told him. "My God, we're both too tall for this thing." Our faces were pressed so close together, I could have counted the hairs on his head.

"Maybe we should've ran," he joked, his warm breath a caress on my ear. I involuntarily shivered.

"To where?" I asked, shaking off the tension of the proximity. "An invisible car?"

We both started laughing at the ludicrousness of our situation. Tom looked at me just then, really looked at me for the first time without guarded eyes.

"You're beautiful, January," he told me.

My eyes widened and my jaw went slack. "Is that a compliment *from you*, Eriksson?"

"I should have told you that first night in Austin."

"Why didn't you?" I asked in a whisper, not believing where this conversation was headed.

"I was a dumbass."

"Really, tell me, Tom. There's something going on with you. Jason told me you used to be this carefree, funny guy. Then it was like a switch went off, he said, and you became this, and I quote, 'hulking beast who hates the world.'"

"He's an idiot," he said, but his grin negated the statement.

"No, he's not. He cares for you."

"Yeah, yeah," he said, meeting my eyes once more. Our breaths came out in billowy clouds. "Wish they'd turn the car on. Are you cold?" he asked.

"Freezing, but it's not like you can warm me up," I said, without thinking.

I caught the surprise in his eyes and my face and neck heated up to its usual unnatural red. "Oh, I could warm you up," he answered, shocking the hell out of me.

"Tom," I said, closing my eyes.

"Come closer," he said, inching my way.

"If I was any closer, I'd be on your lap."

"I have no qualms with that."

"Tom, stop it."

"I'm tired of pretending I don't find you the sexiest girl I've ever met in my entire life."

"Your entire life."

"I'm serious, January. You want to know why I moved to Austin?" When I didn't say anything, he continued. "I moved to get away from a girl I was in love with but she belonged to someone else." I gulped, my stomach twisted in knots. "But when we kissed, that burning need to have her vanished in an instant."

I took another deep breath. "Then why treat me like a disease?"

"I'm afraid of you."

"Afraid."

"I'm a coward, January. I'm not sure if I can handle another heartbreak and I *know* if I fell for you, I'd fall so hard there'd be no coming back from it. You're extraordinary."

I felt my body go still and my heart beat into my throat at his confession. My breaths got deeper and my chest began to pant. "Tom," I whispered. "Sometimes the risk can be worth the reward."

We leaned into one another and closed our eyes. He languidly kissed the side of my red throat. His mouth following up, up, up until he reached my jaw and my breath hitched in my throat.

"I think you may be right, MacLochlainn." He kissed down my jaw line until he came to the hollow beneath my ear. "Do you know how many times I've imagined doing this for the past six months?"

"Oh, God," I panted. "Probably not as many times as I've imagined." I needed my hands free! If they hadn't been tied so well behind my back, they would have been interlaced in his hair, clutching his mouth to mine.

He followed farther up my jaw and across my cheek. I closed my eyes in anticipation as I felt his lips at the corner of my mouth.

"'Ey, lovebirds! Ready for jail?" Officer One teased, settling into the driver's seat. Tom and I broke eye and skin contact to glance his direction. He leaned over his seat toward us. "You really are a strange lot," he said as Officer David opened the passenger side door and sat down.

Tom took a complete one-eighty. "What's the charge, officer?"

"Attempted burglary."

"Ah, I see, and what were we supposedly attempting to steal?"

"Uh," Officer One said, looking over at Officer David. "When we look at the tapes..."

"Oh! They have tapes! Thank God!" I interjected, earning a silencing look from Officer David.

"We should get you attempting to open the register."

"You won't get that at all," Tom said. "And when you find out that we were just innocent in all this, our car stolen, etc. How quickly can we be released?"

"Assuming you're right, which we're not, you'd be out in, oh, say, twelve hours?"

"Twelve hours!" I said. "But we have to be in London by ten!"

"Yeah, London by ten, you say? For what? Probably secret drug meetin's and such."

"Oh, for Heaven's sake!" I said. "We just had use for the phone is all!"

"January," Tom said, shaking his head. "Do we get a phone call at the station?" he asked Officer One.

"One, yes."

At the station, they processed us both by taking our prints followed by a round of mug shots. I glanced at the computer and saw the pic they'd taken and almost burst out laughing. I looked like a frightened rabbit. Truthfully, I was a little frightened, but not enough to deprive myself of the laugh that was my mug shot. Does anyone take a good mug shot?

Tom rang Jason and let him know everything that'd went down. I stood beside him, waiting for my turn to call...someone. Jason would have been my call but Tom took care of that, so I called July.

"Hello?" I heard July's voice and it sounded so good to hear.

"July!"

"January! Oh my God! How are you?"

"Oh, you know, just hangin' out," I said, contorting my face at Tom. He shrugged his shoulders, physically approving of my choice of words. Nice. "Well, I mean, I'm in the slamma here in some little town an hour outside of London, but..."

"*What*! Why! Oh my God, January! What is going on? Do I need to call the Embassy?"

"July, we're in the U.K., not Nicaragua, calm down." Tom laughed.

"Who was that?" July asked.

"Oh, that's Tom," I said, without making eye contact.

"May I speak with him?"

"No."

"Why ever not?"

"Because it's unnecessary. I'm calling you because I've got a free call and you're the only person I could think of to waste it on while they prove we are innocent of all our menacing charges."

"What were you charged with?"

"Murder one."

"Shut up, January," she said, making me smile.

Officer David gave me the sign for "wrap it up." Apparently that signal is universal.

"Uh, I gotta go, buttercup. I love you, okay? I'll call you when I break out. Tell Mom I love her and let her know I'm getting lots and lots of prison tattoos with the name 'Bubba,' or whatever the English equivalent to Bubba is, on my chest and arms."

"Love you too," she said and I hung up.

I walked over to Tom and sat next to him in one of the dirty plastic chairs that lay in several lines, to accommodate the staggering number of men and women, no doubt. I'm being sarcastic. There was one other gentleman in there and he was drunk as a skunk and so far off we could barely see him.

"I take it your sister is well?"

"Very."

"Embassy?"

"Yes, she's a bit...dramatic."

"You don't say?" he said, with a gentle smirk on his face.

"Good news!" We heard behind us. We both stood and faced Officer David. "You've been cleared of all charges. They found ya' car right where you left it. I hadn't looked far enough it seems."

"Oh thank God!" I said, grasping at my chest.

"What can we expect from here?" Tom asked.

"You're free to go, but I'd wait 'ere if I was you. Night's cooled things off a bit. You can use that phone to ring your friend."

"Thank you," Tom said, walking back to the wall phone. He dialed Jason and I waited impatiently beside him, desperate to leave the place. My first impressions of England weren't *impressing*. "Jason?" I heard. "Yeah, we're good, bro. Thanks." Laughing. "Yeah, okay, that's fine, dude. Oh, good, good. All right," he said, glancing at his watch, "cool. Talk to you later."

He hung up.

"What'd he say?" I asked.

"The rental company will deliver a new car here in the next half hour."

"What about our belongings?"

"They'll transfer them into the new vehicle. Apparently they were very apologetic."

"Shall we wait in the lobby near the doors so we can watch for them?"

"That's a great idea," he said with a wink. That wink told me two things. One, he was freaking adorable and did things like wink. The only other person I knew who winked was my grandpa. Two, that he was excited about privacy with...Lil'. Ol'. Me.

He took my hand and guided me through the doors. The officers waved and saluted after apologizing for the misunderstanding. We exited through the heavy double doors with the tiny pocket window, letting it slam against our backs.

"God, I would never want to go to prison," I said.

For some reason, this made Tom laugh. He was doing a lot of that lately. "First off, that was not prison. That wasn't even jail. That was a processing area. And secondly, you could never go to prison because you're too good of a person to go to prison."

"Oh yeah? And how do you know that, huh? The only thing we seem to exchange is saliva." My face literally melted into my neck at that statement, but I pretended it did no such thing.

"I know you're embarrassed, you know."

"Yes, it's a curse."

He stopped me short and swung me in front of him, "It's lovely." Well, if that didn't make me blush harder. *Dang it.* His smile got deeper and he brought his hand up to my face, guiding his hand across my cheek. I sank my face into his palm. "You're lovely, January."

His other hand swept my falling hair off my shoulder. "I should probably take my braid out," I said, fingering the mess it'd become. I broke away for a moment and sat on a bench near the station's glass doors. Tom sat next to me and just watched, seemingly mesmerized.

I pulled the chopstick holding my messy bun up and put it between my teeth so I could unbraid my hair. Once I'd worked out all the kinks with my fingers, I let it all fall to my shoulders. "That feels so much better," I said around the chopstick as I twisted the length around my hand and held it away from my face for a moment.

Tom removed the chopstick from my teeth and stuck it within an inside pocket of his leather jacket before dragging my body closer to his and making me face him. "I'll watch the doors," he said softly, his eyes roaming my head as he laced his big, warm hands through my hair. My eyes became heavy.

"Stop making me sleepy, Thomas Eriksson."

"I can't help it. It's like I *need* to run my fingers through your hair."

"It's my favorite thing in the world," I said lazily before opening my eyes to the most handsome face I'd ever seen in my entire life.

"What?" he asked.

"Nothing, I just..."

There was a knock on the station's glass doors and a young woman in the rental company's uniform waved. We walked over to her and met her on the sidewalk.

"Mister Eriksson?" she asked and he nodded. "I'm so sorry about all this. We've upgraded your vehicle for you for the inconvenience and taken care of your bill. Is there anything else we can do for you?" she asked, handing over the keys.

"None, thank you," Tom answered.

"Just give us a ring, love, if there is," she said with a sweet smile.

"Will do. Again, thank you."

The woman ran to an awaiting car behind us and we climbed into our new rental. It was definitely an upgrade. Like, mega upgrade. It was a giant SUV, the likes of which I'd yet to see in Ireland or England thus far. Land Rover. Score! Jason had done this, I'd known it as soon as I saw it.

Thomas

We reached London in just under an hour. The GPS came in handy, taking us right to The Chesterfield in Mayfair. As we drove up to the hotel, or palace, depending how you looked at it, I was stumped. We both stared in fascination.

"Why would Jason put us here?" I asked no one in particular.

But January answered anyway. "Because he loves us?"

I looked at her in disbelief. "Do you even know Jason?"

She thought for a moment. "You're right. Something's up."

The valet came up and opened the door for January before coming around and taking the keys from me. He informed us in a very formal accent that he'd find out our room and have our bags brought up. "I'll catch you when we leave, bro," I said, letting him know I'd tip him all at once in the end and he nodded tightly.

Inside, the lobby had black-and-white marble floors. Our feet echoed off the walls and pushed back and forth repeatedly, a resounding hymn of clicks. The rest of the room was dark wood and crimson accents, save for the cream plaster ceiling and columns. We approached the Concierge and he greeted us cheerfully, asking our names.

"Thomas Eriksson and January MacLochlainn," I told him. His brows lifted slightly at January, not enough to warrant a beat down but just enough to sting. *Zap*. I felt that simple burn of jealousy for about the hundredth time since being around this girl. If I had any chance of a normal relationship with her, I was going to have to check that quickly. *Relationship? Where the hell did that come from?*

"Yes, sir," he said, clicking away at a computer system. "Ah, yes, I have you both on the third floor, is this acceptable? There are some fantastic views from that room."

"Perfect," January said, before doing a double take. "Wait. Room? Don't you mean *rooms*?"

The man became flustered and peered down at his computer once more. January and I looked at one another, confused.

"No, I'm sorry. You only reserved the one room. Twin beds, though."

"Jason," I said under my breath. "I'm sorry," I said a bit louder, "but we're going to need two rooms."

"I apologize, sir, but there is only the one vacancy."

"It's okay," January said. "It has twin beds, you said?"

"Yes, madam."

"It's all right," January offered, touching me lightly on the arm.

I nodded. "Are you sure?"

"Sure, let's just get out there and listen to some music, Tom. I'm kind of dying to do our job right now."

"All right," I said, wishing I could kiss her in that moment. She made my heart feel lighter than it had in over a year. "Fine," I told the man as he started to ready our keys. I turned back to January. "I'll talk to Jason."

"It's fine," she said, squeezing my forearm through my hoodie.

The concierge finalized everything, handing us our keys and letting us know our bags would be up shortly. He pointed us to the elevator and we got in, but when the doors closed and I pressed the button for the third floor, it felt like someone else took over my body.

I couldn't have stopped myself if I'd tried, I grabbed January briskly and pushed her against the side of the elevator, cupping the back of her head so I wouldn't hurt her. She looked surprised but not at all unwilling, her mouth gaped slightly and held a small grin at the corners. I eyed her fiercely before physically turning her head and moving to her beautiful neck. I breathed her beguiling scent deep within my chest. I righted her face and drank her in before closing my eyes and pressing my lips gently to hers. It was everything in me to keep it soft, my body had other ideas, rougher ideas, and wanted so badly to kiss her harshly to release all the pent up feeling I'd been harboring for the fascinating female since that night in Austin.

"I'm into you," I told her as I broke free.

"Are you," she whispered as a statement rather than a question.

"That's a lie," I amended.

Her breaths puffed gently as her eyes wandered my face. "A lie."

"Yes," I said, running my fingers along her neck and throat, resting my palm over her heart, feeling it race for me.

"I'm obsessed with you."

"Ob-obsessed," she said, tripping on the word.

"Am I scaring you?" I asked, removing my hand from her chest and bringing it back to her throat.

The elevator door dinged, alerting us to our floor and we both stepped out without another word spoken. I opened the door with the electronic key and let her in first. When the door closed, I held fast to her arm and whipped her back to me, pinning her once again against the door. The only light in the room was a soft lamp in the corner.

"No," she said.

"No, what?"

"No, you're not scaring me."

"I can't stop thinking about you," I acknowledged to her as well as myself. My stare raked her body from her feet to the top of her head. "Want to hear something damaged?"

"Always."

"I dream about you."

"Dream."

"Yes, all the time. Every night. Every single night, January."

"About what?"

"It wouldn't be...prudent for me to say," I admitted, not believing I admitted to it.

She giggled timidly and I could feel her face and neck pitch to a feverish degree. "Stop," I spoke into her hair.

"I can't help it," she whimpered, sending me in every different direction possible.

"Then be prepared."

"For what?"

"For this," I said, pressing my body severely into hers.

She groaned and I almost let go of all self-control at that captivating sound. Her long legs climbed up mine and I very nearly tossed her to one of the impossibly small twin beds. Her fingers combed through my hair and pulled slightly at the ends, bringing the kiss deeper.

"Tom," she breathed into my mouth.

"Hmm?" I asked, moving to her jaw and throat.

"The door, Tom." She said at the knocking behind her.

"What?" I asked, pulling away, supremely pissed that we had luggage that even needed bringing to us.

I let her incredible body slide down mine until her feet hit the floor. I made sure she held up before flipping on the light, running my hands through my hair and taking a deep breath. I opened the door and a bellhop brought our duffels in, laying them against the wall near the television.

I gave him a few pounds, thanked him and he left.

"Whoa," she said, the backs of her hands at her cheeks.

"I know, I shouldn't have let it get that far. I'm sorry."

"Well that too," she said, her face bright red. My lids became hooded and she brought her hand to her throat. "Sorry," she whispered. "I meant 'Whoa, this room.' It's like the British Navy threw up in here!"

I looked around and finally saw what she did. "Cripes! You're right. I'm blind!"

"Gah! All bright blue and gold! What were they thinking?" She laughed and I couldn't help but join her.

"It is ridiculous."

I glimpsed at the nightstand and read the time. "Crap!"

"What?"

"It's nine-fifteen."

"No!"

"Listen," I said, "don't forget this, okay? I need you to remember that kiss. I want you to know that I do still very much want you."

Her face bloomed in answer.

"Just give me a moment," she said. "I'll be ready in fifteen. You can get ready in here, if you want?" I nodded. "I'll, uh, knock on the inside of the bathroom door when I'm ready to make sure you're dressed."

I heard water running for a moment and sounds of cloth hitting the sink and floor, including her shoes. I placed my hand on the door and closed my eyes, praying that God gave me the patience to sleep in the same room with that magnificent creature.

I was going to kill Jason.

I unpacked everything in the duffel in the set of drawers nearest the bed at the window. I knew we were only going to be there a day, but if you've ever had to live out of a duffel, you know it's harder than living out of a suitcase. If you don't keep everything organized and folded, it can take you hours to make it right again.

I threw on a pair of jeans and thermal under yet another black t-shirt before shrugging on my hoodie. I stood in front of a mirror and ran my hands through my hair. Done. I walked to the closet near the bathroom and removed the provided laundry bag, throwing all my stuff from that day and the day before inside.

I knocked on the bathroom door. A tiny shriek came from inside, making me laugh. "I'm not decent!" she said.

"Oh well, then it's okay for me to come in then."

"No! Not decent! *Not* decent!" I was quiet for a minute. "You're kidding me, aren't you?"

I didn't answer, just laughed. "January, here's the laundry bag for all your stuff. I'll set it right outside the door. We'll want to have our things laundered tomorrow since we'll be out of here tomorrow evening."

Chapter Seven

At Least I'm Not as Sad

Thomas

January emerged fifteen minutes later, looking for all the world like sex on heels and I tried desperately to pretend she didn't. We both moved in front of the sink and brushed our teeth together, trying not to laugh in the mirror and get toothpaste down our fronts, but that didn't really work out too well for me.

A fresh t-shirt later, and we were out the door. January, a walking, ticking time bomb and I, the detonator. It was only a matter of time before one of two things happened. Either some idiot was going to push me over the line, or she was. I imagined both wouldn't exactly be ideal. Though, I did have a preference.

"You know what you're doing," I told her as we settled into the scene of the only crime we'd actually committed that night. Yeah, I did that.

"Whatever do you mean?" She feigned surprise, her hand flew to her chest.

"You know what you look like. You'd have to be an idiot not to and you, January MacLochlainn, are not an idiot."

"What?" She teased, one brow raised. "Do you plan those little ditties out before hand, or was that off the cuff?"

"I apologize, was that not clever enough for you?"

"It was beneath you, Eriksson, beneath you."

"I know something else I'd like beneath me," I joked.

She laughed loudly, her laugh the equivalent of a ringing bell, before checking herself. "See? You just killed it. It's literally dead, floating upside down and bloated. It's that dead."

"What a visual. You're the queen of defusing sexual tension."

She made a tiny bow, raising the hem of her skirt a little and sending me very near that edge I warned you about. "Thank you. Thank you," she said, righting herself. "Don't try this at home, folks. I'm a professional."

"You're an idiot."

"Thomas Eriksson! You've cut me to the core! I don't believe I can go on," she said with an exaggerated Southern accent. She leaned her body against mine and went limp. I gladly held her up and against me. "Tell Mama I love her. Tell July I bequeath to her my collection of shells from around the world, and the snow globes can go to August." She died in my arms and then peeked up at me with one eye open as the doors slid wide to a packed lobby.

A woman gasped at our position but caught herself before making too much of a scene. Can't express too loudly her distaste in us or she would be too closely associated. The remainder of her party looked equally repulsed and that was just comical to me. They were disgusted for just one reason and it had nothing to do with who we were but *what we weren't.*

"Don't look now, MacLochlainn, but I believe we may be shocking these folks with our radical clothing and complete lack of personal space." *And obvious lack of money.*

She peered their direction and stood up, smoothing down her skirt and raising her chin to the level of "I don't care what you think of me," but it did nothing to convince me because her neck was painted a bright red. I hated that she felt embarrassed by being silly, funny, herself. Hated that. Who did they think they were? She was probably infinitely more intelligent than these lemmings as well as talented as hell. She had absolutely nothing to be humiliated about. She was amazing.

I grabbed her hand and we strode confidently through the lobby and out the doors.

"January, can I be candid with you?

"Hmm? Of course," she said, distracted.

"I find you to be...extraordinary."

"You do?" she said, a genuine smile touching the corner of her eyes.

"Hell yes, I do. One of the most."

"Thank you, Tom. That's very kind of you to say."

"It's not kind, it's the truth. Come on," I said, wrapping her underneath my arm as we headed for the Tube toward London's Soho district.

We were headed for Ronnie Scott's. That's where The Mark were scheduled to play first at ten. Seven didn't dictate who we watched or even when or where, but if they made a suggestion, I was going to accommodate, especially if Jonah could be there. Which reminded me.

"If Jonah's there, we have to play it cool with this," I said, lifting her hand in mine.

"Okay," she said, a bit hurt.

"It's not because I don't want to shout about it and shit. It's because if Jonah found out, word would get out and you could jeopardize solidifying a position as a scout, January. I would feel awful if that happened."

"Oh, okay." She said, still sounding disappointed.

"Hey," I said, pulling her short. I placed my hands on either side of her neck to drive the point home. "I swear, January, I'm so into you it's not even funny. I just can't compromise you like that. You're obviously going to earn scout by your own merit, but if anyone at Seven thinks it's because we've gotten together, no one will take you seriously. I just can't have that. You're too good for that."

Her eyes crinkled in a smile. "And what is 'this'?"

"Huh?"

"You said we had to play it cool with 'this.' What is 'this,' Tom?"

"It's the beginning, January."

"Of what?" she asked me seriously.

"We'll have all the time in the world to talk about that. It's too deep to get into it right now but know this, I'm tired of pretending. So weary of it. I forgot myself when I lost who I thought Kelly was to me, but you've shown me what I think, no, I *know* no one else could have shown me."

"And what's that?"

"That I don't want to be lost anymore. I - I want *you*."

She kissed me then and my tongue found hers. She smacked of innocence and saccharinelike want. Two of the most appetizing flavors I'd ever tasted and knew I'd never get enough of. January was who I wanted and I'd realized in that moment that she eclipsed Kelly with the power of a thousand suns. Thank God for unanswered prayers.

I dragged her with me through Ronnie Scott's door and squeezed her hand before letting go. We both searched the crowd for Jonah but didn't see him.

"He's not here," she said.

"Who's not?" A deep timbre asked her. I fought with myself not to tuck January into my side.

"Jonah," I said, turning around and offering my hand.

"Tom," he said, shaking the hand I'd offered. "January!" He exclaimed dropping my hand like it was diseased and picking January up, swinging her around. "It's been so long, sweet."

"Jonah," January acknowledged with a wry smile, pushing herself off his chest. "Stop showing off. I just saw you in New York last week."

Jonah set her down and I resisted the urge to punch him in the face. *He can't cross a boundary he doesn't know exists.* "I'm sorry. Eight days is too long when it comes to your face," he laid on thickly, grabbing her jaw with one hand and rubbing his thumb across her cheek. January rolled her eyes but laughed.

"Shall we lay it all out?" Jonah asked us both.

"Go on," I said, folding my arms across my chest.

"I'm gonna win," he said, smiling.

I laughed quietly and shook my head. "No, you won't."

"We'll see," he said, slapping me on the back as if it was all in good fun.

He kissed January's cheek and lifted two fingers above his head as he walked away.

"I'm really starting to hate that guy," I admitted.

"I like Jonah. I really do, but he can do some douchey things. I'm just warning you."

"What?" I asked, turning to face her.

"Seriously. I heard he was doing some sketchy things when it came to bands."

"Well, like what?"

She raised her hands in the air as if in surrender. "Listen, I don't want to start shit, but I heard he was paying an insider at Seven under the table to find out where you would be scouting. Again!" She said, grabbing my shoulder. "I really don't want to start anything. I just think we should be careful."

"Damn it!" I exclaimed. "Why didn't you say anything before?"

"Don't shoot the messenger, dude! Plus, I thought it would've been obvious to you since he's at almost every show you're at."

"Dude, I *knew* that was too much a coincidence. I gave him the benefit of the doubt."

"For someone being so cynical in love, you sure are naive about life."

"Shut it, MacLochlainn."

January laughed. "Zipping it."

While the first band set up, January and I took a seat at the bar together. People milled in and around us but we ignored them.

"What'll you have?" the bartender asked us.

"Strawberry mojito," January said without any prompt from me.

"Whatever you have on tap," I said.

The bartender nodded and left to make our drinks.

"Strawberry mojito?" I asked, trying not to laugh.

"Shut up, Eriksson. All the girls at work rant and rave about strawberry mojitos and I found myself in a situation where I can try one. I'm a newbie. Cut me some slack."

"All right, all right. I hope you like it."

"Thank you," she said, bowing her head.

We both turned around in our stools to face the crowd and the stage. I placed my hand on her knee absently to lean into her ear.

"Careful," January teased before I could speak. "If Jonah sees this he could read into it."

"Sorry," I said, lifting my hand but kept my mouth at her ear. "Can you see him?" I asked her, changing direction.

She turned her head to the left slightly then the right. "No, he's chatting up some broad with huge boobs. Totally immersed. In conversation, not her boobs," she said, clarifying.

I laughed in her ear, sending goose bumps up her neck. "I forgot what I was going to say now. You can't be funny when I'm trying to be sexy with you."

"Don't you know?" she asked me, her throat vibrating as she laughed. "Funny *is* sexy."

"Of course, everyone knows *that,* but *I'm* the one who's trying to be sexy. You can't over-sexy me. You're outdoing my attempt at sexy. It's not fair."

"I apologize," she teased, leaning into me, but keeping an eye on Jonah. "Try, try again."

"January." I repeated her name because nothing had ever felt better to say, especially in that moment.

I trailed my lips down the back of her neck, inciting a shiver. I placed one slow, soft kiss on the spot where my lips lingered and sat back up. January's eyes closed briefly and she pitched forward slightly sending a strange sensation of approval up my spine at the way I affected her. I fixed my posture and looked toward the stage area as the band was readying to play.

"They're on," I told her, glancing Jonah's direction. His eyes searched the crowd before stopping at us. He lazily saluted me in acknowledgment before focusing back on the band.

"That's right, ya' bastard. You smile now," I told him under my breath.

Ronnie Scott's was a fairly intimate venue, suited best for acoustic sets. What I hoped was that the band we were about to see was better plugged in than out and that Jonah wouldn't be able to see this.

"Watch for it," I told January.

"For what?"

"When The Mark starts to play, listen to their acoustic set and let me know if you can imagine their set in full instruments. It will always be different. Our job is to decipher whether this band can handle full-fledged or if they're strictly acoustic. Occasionally, I'll have to ask to see them again. It's why I avoid acoustic sets like the plague."

"Oh, I see. Okay, I'll try that. Why do you avoid acoustic sets?"

"Because live gigs with ten thousand people don't sound that great when your instrument can't reach them."

"'Kay."

"We have an advantage because we're already familiar with them. Ten to one, so is Jonah."

From the first strum, I'd had The Mark, well, marked and by the look on January's face, so did she.

"Caged," she said, repeating her first diagnosis.

"Exactly," I agreed. "Shall we? There are a few bands playing at The Garage."

"Cool."

We waved at Jonah on our way out. He politely waved back but the look of bewilderment was enough to send us both over the edge when we reached the path outside.

"He looked so confused," January said into her hand.

"Like a lost puppy, that Jonah."

"He should really do his own research," she offered by way of explanation.

"No, when he did that, he picked wrong. That's why he cheats."

"Where's The Garage?" she hedged.

"A good twenty minutes that direction by way of the Tube." I pointed northeast. "But it's worth it. Lots of good bands playing tonight."

"How do you know?" she asked.

"I arranged it."

"What?" she asked, eyes wide.

"I phoned the manager of the place, told him who I was, well, I may have fabricated my exact position with Seven, but it was all for prosperity mind you, and I got him to book four bands I've been dying to hear from the area."

"You're pulling my leg!"

"No, I'm definitely not." My hands would tremble anywhere near her legs.

"That's amazing! Why'd we even bother at Ronnie Scott's?"

"Ah, that reason is twofold. You see, Jonah needed to know we were here and that we were only attending The Mark's performance to appease the label and that we had better things hidden up our sleeves."

"That's three reasons."

"No, I lumped the last two in as one."

"Oh, I see. Well, lead the way, my diabolical master."

"This way," I told her. "Next week's lesson? How to execute a fiendish cackle while drumming the fingers."

"Will I need any supplies for the lesson?"

"No, just be sure to rest your voice the night before."

"Done."

The Garage was packed beyond belief and I wondered if Jonah was going to show up after all, seeming as it must have been advertised well or perhaps it was word of mouth. I was hoping the latter.

Performances:

Georgia Asher - Unique in her songs and performance. Highly entertaining.
Influences: Janelle Monae, Fun.
My take: Great musician, contract immediately.
January's take: "Awesome musician, contract immediately."

One Lump Or Two - No Doubt rip off. Great live performance.
My take: No way.
January's take: "Sorry, two thumbs down."

Compass - Strange instrumentals. Live performance lacking.
My take: Could be good if they added a few more traditional pieces.
January's take: "No way, Jose."

Let Them Eat Cake - Female vocalist. An actual decent female vocalist. Possibility of going commercial.
My take: Yeah, they could clean up their sound and go commercial, but they're so damn good why bother?

Suppose we should let them decide.

January's take. "Tom, if you have Jason offer it to them, let them know they probably won't sound the same. Plus, there's no guarantee they'll be accepted commercially still."

"If they went commercial, January, they would be accepted and well."

"I disagree."

"I know a little of what I'm talking about. They'd be a massive hit."

"You're going to poison the one thing that gives them their edge, though."

"I'm not so sure. I think it can transcend. Only time will tell."

"Fine. Call Jason. Ruin them," she joked with a smile.

"Do you even remember who signs your paychecks?" I teased.

"Shit. I forgot that for a second. Yes, call Jason but let him know that he needs to replace their keyboardist."

"Really?" I asked her. "Why?"

"Because he's terrible," she said, laughing.

"Egad. I couldn't tell from their set. Well, I suppose that instrument is your forte. You would know."

"Thomas Eriksson is conceding a point? Just a moment." She picked up an imaginary cell. "Yes. Oh, it has? Well then, I see." She hung up. "It's official, hell's frozen over."

"What are you talking about? I'm a reasonable person," I told her as we headed toward the Tube.

"Oh, yes, extremely reasonable. You forget you treated me like crap the first time we met," she admitted, the teasing leaving her tone.

"That's not fair, January. I apologized for that already."

"Sure," she smirked disbelievingly with a twist at her lips.

"Hey," I said softly, turning her toward me. "I don't think you understand what was going on with me."

"I knew what happened. I'm just saying I find it utter bull that you used that as an excuse to shit on everyone around you."

"January, I don't think you understand what you do to me."

"Explain it."

"Let's get to the hotel first. It's cold and late and I want you safe."

We traveled in silence, all the way to our hotel, I still wrapped my arm around her shoulder and she didn't shrug it off which made me think she just wanted to work through what was going on. I understood it. I was a confusing bastard. One minute, I was a complete asshole, the next I was practically confessing an undying infatuation. Emotional whiplash.

The ride up the elevator stirred the heat I'd let go dormant. The memory of how her soft flesh felt pressed to mine sent waves of pleasure up my spine. I glanced her direction and her eyes were as dark as mine with the same recollection.

"No," I laughed. "Don't look at me like that, January. This is hard enough without you looking like a bowl of ice cream."

"I've a spoon, Tom."

"Shut up. Seriously, I'm not joking. I need to get this off my chest. I need parameters."

"Parameters? Attraction doesn't have parameters."

"No, attraction doesn't but potential does."

That shut her right up and I nearly laughed at her wide-eyed expression. I let us into the room and we kind of roamed around, pretending to do things, avoiding the inevitable conversation. Finally, I sat on the side of one of the beds and slid to the carpet below. She followed suit and sat opposite me on the floor, our legs touching. I fiddled with the zipper of my hoodie, afraid to look her way. *Jeez, dude, grow a pair and talk to her.*

"January," I began, looking directly in her eyes. "I've never regretted anything so much as the way I treated you the night we first kissed." She was smiling at first but sucked in a breath at my proclamation. "I was, *is,* really, in a strange place. My chest ached perpetually and I unfairly and immaturely took that out on everyone I met, especially you.

"When we met, I was six months into a self-inflicted prison sentence."

"What happened?" she asked timidly.

I breathed deeply, leaning my head on the side of the bed. "There was a girl. Kelly. She'd been a part of our group for years and years. We were best friends but I never looked at her that way. I mean, sure, she was hot as hell, but Kelly wasn't someone I wanted to touch. She was *Kelly*. Get me?" I asked her.

She nodded gingerly.

"I was in a band and that meant all that it implies. I dated hundreds of girls. Kissed thousands. Did...other things." I ran my hands over my face at the confession. "I'm not proud of who I was. I was young and stupid." I peered her direction, her face held only anticipation. "Not exactly the best excuse, I know, but I thought I was doing everything right, getting tested regularly, being careful, blah, blah, blah, but a year and a half ago, I couldn't pretend anymore that it was at all fulfilling." I ran my hand through my hair, tucking the strands behind my ears. "I was disgusted with myself, to be honest. I'd seen everything that world could offer and I was only twenty-two. Suddenly, it was like a switch flipped and I saw Kelly for the real woman she was and my God was I ever in love with her."

January's chest panted, her face flushed and her eyes glassed, making me feel terrible. I didn't want to make her uncomfortable, but she needed to know why I was the way I'd become...I wasn't finished.

"Wait, January," I told her, grabbing her hand.

"I'm listening," she choked.

"But I was too late. She met and became engaged to someone else."

"Oh dear," January said, confusing me. I squeezed her hand to let me finish.

"And I hated every fiber of his being. He was wealthy, connected, educated, and, unfortunately, sincerely in love with her in return. It ate at me. At first, I'd indulged in women but that proved useless. My ache only got deeper. I was thoroughly ashamed of myself because I'd begun to subtly infiltrate their relationship, demanding she see films and go to restaurants with me. I figured, hell, she wasn't married yet, she was fair game, but even I knew how wrong that was. It was all under the pretense of friendship. I was being dishonest with her.

"When her fiancé called our little meetings off for us, that's when I fled to Austin."

"And that's where you met me."

"That's when I met you."

"I see now," she said sadly.

"No, you don't, January. You really don't."

"Tell me then."

"I just wanted to forget Kelly, wanted her out of my mind and chest and I wanted no one to ever be able to get within five feet of me for reasons I think obvious. Dude, I thought I could never hurt so badly as I did when I realized that I could never have Kelly...but..."

"But?" she asked, unknowingly inching forward.

I spoke quietly, almost too quietly, afraid to admit it out loud. I closed my eyes tightly. "But that hurt was nothing in comparison to how badly I'd begun to feel when a stranger kissed me in a dusty lot just six months ago."

"Jesus, I'm so sorry, Tom," she exclaimed, her back falling against the side of her bed.

"What the hell for?"

"I shouldn't have done what I did," she said, her eyes glassing over.

"Yes, you should have, January."

"No, I shouldn't have." She dropped her eyes to her lap and I could actually feel the sadness radiate from her.

I sat up on my knees and brought her up with me, bringing her face inches from mine. "Don't ever say that, January. You revived me. You *saved* me. You did what I'm convinced no other person could have done and believe me they'd tried. As badly as I hurt for Kelly, it was nothing, *nothing* in comparison to how I felt when I didn't do right by that total stranger. January, you eclipse Kelly! I'm ashamed to say it, but this friend I was convinced I loved is nothing compared to you. I feel like a fool. I could have sworn when I lost Kelly that I lost my soul mate but I was so wrong. So, so wrong."

She shook her head. She needed convincing? Fine.

"I didn't know you from Adam, but God how I dreamt of you night after night after night. You were this ghost I carried along with me everywhere I went, overshadowing the hate I carried for what Kelly didn't even really do to me. If Jason hadn't called me to New York, I know I would have come searching you out. I was obsessed with you and I barely knew you." I searched her face. "Doesn't that scare you?"

"No," she said calmly.

"Why the hell not?" I asked, bewildered. "This infatuation I have for you is borderline psychotic, even I recognize that."

"Because," she said, swallowing. "Because I'd be lying if I said I didn't feel it too. I feel desperate when it comes to you. Desperate and a little bit insane. All I can think about around you is what you taste like."

"Don't tell me things like that," I begged her. I squeezed my eyes closed and rested my forehead against hers, fighting control with every grit of my teeth.

"Why? It's only the truth."

"You don't know me."

"I know enough."

With each word she'd spoken, the growing, bubbling tension spilled between us. Her eyes grew wide when she realized what was about to happen, how I was about to take out everything I'd ever kept inside for the past year on her small, beautiful face but she didn't break away. No, she crept even closer so I slammed my mouth to hers, breathing her in so deeply, I swear I could feel her heartbeat on my tongue. My hands held her jaw and as softly as I could manage, I guided her to her feet, never breaking our kiss. I trailed my fingers down her neck, to her backside and lifted her. She wrapped her incredibly long legs around my waist and I fell to the bed behind me.

We sat there, trading sighs, trading wants, trading intentions. It seemed so incredibly inevitable to me then, how our lives were going to be forever entwined. I knew this was the last person I'd ever kiss, could feel it in my bones, and it was with January MacLochlainn, the most amazing girl I'd ever laid eyes on.

Was I in love with January MacLochlainn? No, I couldn't say I was...but I was going to be. Make no mistake about that.

January

Thomas Eriksson was the last first kiss I was ever going to have. I don't know how I knew it but I could feel it in my bones. A delicious symphony resounded through my head, swum down my body and back through, over and over. The soundtrack to what our life was to become played beautifully around us and I wasn't afraid. And I could tell, neither was he.

We fit so incredibly well together, it was borderline painful.

Our make out session wound down to a comfortably slow back and forth, our lips achingly raw but neither of us feeling the pain. His light stubble scratched at my chin and I reveled in that feeling. I was kissing a man. The idea made me stupidly giddy inside as if I had any real idea what that really meant. All I knew was I had moved on from a "never" mentality to a very solid "please, please, please" one. I held on to his hoodie tightly between both hands, too frightened to unclench them and draw down his zipper, all his zippers. *Do it, January*, I ordered myself.

But Tom drew away from me slowly, peppering my neck with soft kisses that made me melt from the inside out. My heart and guts were a soft, liquefied mess and I loved the sensation.

"It's late," he whispered hoarsely. The deeper octave sending shivers up my spine.

"So what," I offered, drawing his lips back to mine.

"Not 'so what,'" he said, chuckling against my mouth, making me laugh along with him. "Come on, love. Let's sleep."

"Sleep?" I asked in disbelief.

"Yes, I must save you from me. Another minute and you'd be in peril, Miss MacLochlainn."

"I like a bit of danger, though," I said sleepily, as he brought me to his chest.

I felt it shake beneath me. "I imagine you'd be quite the daredevil, actually."

"I've a beautiful cape I could wear," I teased.

"Shut up," he snickered. "Sleep, January," he said, a final kiss at my temple.

And I did, but somewhere in the back of my mind, I could have sworn he'd whispered, "You're too beautiful to sully,"

I woke to Thomas talking on the phone, to Jason it sounded like. "Georgia Asher, yeah, definitely want her immediately. She's versatile enough that she'd be welcomed internationally with absolutely no problem. What? Oh, uh, Let Them Eat Cake, but they're not as commercial as Seven usually likes. You might have to finesse them a bit." Pregnant pause. "No, I told you, forget about The Mark, Jonah is wrong. Okay, but don't say I didn't warn ya'. Yeah, I'll tell her. Bye."

I felt his cell phone drop on the bed as soft swishes of cloth slid into the bottom of his duffel. I turned over and stretched out, my legs practically shot two feet off the end of my bed.

"How did we both sleep on this tiny nothing," I said out loud, my voice hoarse from disuse.

"Well, that leg was wrapped around mine," he said, pointing to each part as he continued his explanation, "that stomach was pressed to mine, that beautiful face was buried in my neck. It was the best and worst night's sleep of my life." I smiled. "Good morning," he said, smiling back.

"Morning, Tom. How much time do we have?"

"'Bout an hour."

"I'm gonna shower then."

"All right, I'll go check out downstairs while you do that."

"Thank you," I told him, kissing his cheek as I trudged toward the shower.

Chapter Eight
Take A Picture

January

We were on the road and headed toward the Channel Tunnel an hour later. I made sure I had all my meds with me but Tom assured me the ride was exponentially smoother than a water voyage and it would take us straight to Paris in only two and a half hours. I knew Europe was small but it was flabbergasting to think I could go from London to Paris in the time it takes to watch a film. Okay, the film would be *Lord of the Rings: The Fellowship of the Ring*, but still, that's pretty amazing.

We dropped the car off at the rental place and cabbed it over to the Chunnel station. The entire process from leaving the hotel to boarding the train took less than an hour. I was impressed, thoroughly. Impressed because everything we did in Texas seemingly took a day's commitment. One, because everything is twenty miles away regardless of where you're going but also, to be honest, we just move slower than the rest of the world. It's why we're incorrectly pegged as slower thinkers. We aren't. In fact, we're sharper than most people; we just take our time, fewer mistakes that way. I think I sort of preferred it that way, but a little change of pace was always nice. Always.

We boarded the Eurostar and easily found our seats.

"Comfortable?" Tom asked.

"Very," I said, laying my head on his shoulder and whipping out a bag of Twizzlers I brought from home. "Want one?

"Always." He reached into the bag and pulled out a vine. That's when I noticed it.

"Your jacket's unzipped."

"So it is," he said, glancing down at himself, not realizing the significance.

His t-shirt was plain as day. He slumped a bit in his seat making it stretch tightly over his stomach. He'd chosen a charcoal grey tee and it was light enough for me to count each individual muscle in his abdomen. My own stomach clenched in the need to outline each one.

"My God," I blurted, unaware I'd said it out loud.

"What?" he asked absently, chewing his Twizzler.

"Oh," I gulped, "nothing. I, uh, just-nothing."

"*Okay,*" he sung, narrowing his brows in suspicion.

"Want to listen to my iPod with me?" I asked. It was very important that I changed the subject.

"For business or pleasure?" he asked.

"Purely pleasure," I said, my face and neck warming to a deep crimson. I could feel it burn up my neck slowly. I leaned into my bag in front of me to retrieve my iPod, letting my hair fall.

"Your hair has a bit of split, January. I can see your skin."

"Damn it," I said, blushing deeper, fighting a grin and sitting up.

He leaned into the side of my face and tucked my hair behind my ear. "Not to mention the heat I can feel just emanating off you."

"What?" I panted, turning toward him.

"I can feel it when you blush. It settles here," he said, bringing my hand to his chest. "And here." He brought my hand down the abdomen I wanted to line with my fingers.

I yanked my hand back as if it was on fire, making him laugh loudly.

"Shh," a little old English lady told him over her shoulder.

"Sorry," he said, but the decibel of his laughter did nothing but rise. "Sorry," he said again as the lady stared harder. He choked and coughed into his hand to control himself. "Sorry, ma'am." She turned around. "You're going to get me in trouble, January," he whispered.

"Me? You can't do things like that, Tom. Seriously."

"Why not? That blush of yours drives me up the wall. If I can't see it at least once morning, noon, and night, I don't feel complete."

"Oh, shut up," I said, blushing yet again. "Stupid blood."

"No, it never lies," he said more seriously. "I love your blood, it paints the most beautiful things on your face."

"It doesn't," I told him, rubbing at my cheeks.

"Yes, it does," he said, grabbing my face. His thumbs grazed over my jaw, back and forth, back and forth. He mesmerized me. "It tells me just how much I affect you and, in turn, you enchant me. You're breathtaking, January."

He drew his fingers through my hair roughly and cupped my face in his palms, but he didn't lean in for a kiss like I expected him to. Instead, he brought those hands across my face and down my neck to my shoulders then back up.

"And what a beautiful canvas to paint."

The conductor came over the speaker and spoke in French before relaying the same message in heavily accented English.

"I have no idea what he just said," Tom said, shrugging his shoulders

"He welcomed us aboard and mentioned that it's thirteen twenty-three now and that we should be arriving at Gare Du Norde at approximately sixteen forty-seven in the afternoon."

"What? How in the world did you understand that?" Tom asked, bewildered.

"I speak French," I told the window, staring at the deck as we departed the station.

"You *speak French*?"

"Yeah, I didn't tell you that?" I turned to him, confused at myself.

"No, you failed to mention that you're bilingual."

"Oh, I'm not bilingual," I told him, a smirk tugging at my lips.

"No?"

"I'm *multi*lingual. I speak four languages."

Tom stared at me as if he didn't believe me. He couldn't look away; he stared hard into my eyes begging for an explanation.

"It's not a big deal. Kids are sponges," I offered. He still didn't understand. "I wanted to work for the U.N. as a translator when I was little, so during the summers I learned different languages. It was worth it because it comes in handy though I'd *never* work for the U.N. now."

"Amazing."

"Meh, not so much, I learned some crazy things about the United Nations and decided they weren't exactly the..."

"I wasn't calling the U.N. amazing, January. I was calling *you* amazing. *You're* amazing. Incredible, actually. Every time you make me forget that you're extraordinary with your down-to-earth ways, something else blindsides me and reminds me just how out of my league you really are."

I sat up a bit and scooted closer into his side. I could not believe what he'd just said. I grabbed his arm and leaned into his body. I needed him to feel what he needed to hear. "*You're* out of *my* league? You've got to be joking, Tom."

"Hell no, I'm not joking. You are way out of my league, January."

"This is going to be a problem, I can tell," I teased him.

"It is?"

"Yes, because you keep forgetting what an incredible musician you are and how talented you are at your job. How everyone in this business calls Seven, desperate to contact you so they can steal you away. You're a rock star, yet you're oblivious to it because you're always on the road. It's stupid, but it is what it is. Trust me, Thomas Eriksson, I play in the minors and you're the hypothetical starting pitcher for a team who won the World Series five years consecutive. You're so big league it makes my head spin."

He grinned at me. "That's utter bullshit but I love you for saying it."

I opened my mouth to argue with him but he stopped

me by pressing his lips to mine and I forgot my own name let alone whatever argument I had.

The English countryside held enough charms to distract us from conversation. We fell into a comfortable silence save for our shared earbuds. We listened to the entire *Aim and Ignite* album. The only contact we made was physical. Tom lined my palms with his index finger over and over, making me sleepier than my medicine was.

When we entered France, he nudged me in the ribs. "All the graffiti's in French."

"Imagine that," I teased him.

It got quiet again as we examined the new countryside.

"Talk to me," I told him, breaking the silence.

"What do you want to know?"

"About your family."

"Which one?" He smiled, and the sun gleamed brightly over his white smile.

"The one you grew up with."

"Well, my parents have lived in New York City for most of their lives. They met in a Greenwich Village shop where they'd go to get coffee every morning before work. They married six months later but couldn't conceive right away."

"That's sad. Were they trying?"

"Yeah, they said they just went with it though and were surprised with the news they were pregnant with my sister Christina five years into their marriage. They didn't think it was possible. Then I came along three months after Christina was born."

"Oh, dear. You were a surprise, then."

"You could say that," he told me, grinning.

He took his soda from the chair back in front of him, uncapped it and took a swig. The movement of his throat swallowing made me want to instantly become something edible and sweet so I could slide down his body in an ultimate connection. My fingers tightened on the arms of my chair and I shivered the thought away as I watched him place it back.

"Anyway," he continued, bringing me back to the present, "I have one more sister named Chloe. She's your age and at the Art Institute of Dallas actually."

"What's Christina up to?"

"She's in PR in Manhattan. She's married to a pretty good guy."

"What his name?"

"Pierre. He's French." He snapped at an idea. "I have the best idea. When I introduce you to my parents, you can translate the private conversations between my sister and her husband. It drives the family crazy." My heart beat frantically at the thought that he expected me to meet his family. "Wait," he thought out loud, "you'll probably just join them against us. Never mind, I change my mind." He smiled at me.

"Your sister speaks French?" I asked, hoping I didn't give away my ridiculous excitement that he saw a future with me.

"Yeah, they met during college. Her university had a campus abroad in Paris. Enough said." I smiled at him. "My mom and dad are both teachers."

"Cool. And what are their names?" I asked him.

"Walter and Michelle, but you can call my pops Walt." He fiddled with the zipper of his jacket, seemingly nervous. "I've wanted to ask you something, January, but I wasn't sure how to ask."

"Just say it," I prodded him with my shoulder.

"I'm going back to the States for a week for Kelly's wedding and I-I thought maybe, if you want, you could come as my date?"

I shifted uncomfortably in my seat. I didn't know how to answer this. I did want to go with him to New York, I really did, but it was just too freaking weird knowing I'd be meeting all his friends as he watched the girl he just recently considered the lost love of his life get married. I mean, yeah, he said she meant nothing anymore but no one can just shut off like that and he hadn't even gotten an opportunity to get over her properly.

Suddenly I realized I needed to be very careful.

"Shit," I heard him say, breaking me from my thoughts.

"What?"

"I've scared you off, I can tell."

"No, it's just-it feels weird you asking me to see Kelly get married. I don't know her, but I feel this weird thing for her. I don't like her."

This made Tom laugh. "Baby girl," he said with a bit of his inherited Texas lingo. He picked up my hand and kissed the back. "If I have to spend the next month convincing you she's nothing to me, I'll do it. She doesn't even hold a candle to you, MacLochlainn."

Thomas

The Windmill Festival was just a few days before Kelly's wedding, but we weren't going to Paris just to sit around and wait. The label bought us rail passes to pal around Europe, allowing us to check out as many bands as possible. We were starting in Paris because I wanted January to see the band Jamaica and a few of their starting lineups the next night. I'd planned on working our way through Europe by rail until the festival and then head straight home for the wedding, which surprisingly the thought of didn't affect me at all. I didn't even feel a dull ache. It was as if my body had forgotten all about Kelly and I knew I had January to thank for that.

Damn, that girl was incredible. *Zap*.

I had a week to convince her to come with me. She was coming home with me. She was definitely coming home with me.

The next night, we waited in line to see Jamaica.

"Did Jason talk to Georgia Asher?" she asked me.

"I think so. I hope it went well. She's going to be huge and I hope we get credit for her."

"We will," she told me, her smile reaching her eyes.

I studied her. "You have really beautiful lips, January."

She shyly pinched them together, a red flush crept across her face. I grabbed her face and brought those lips to mine until they were loose again and she kissed me back.

When we pulled apart, her eyes widened and she fought a smile.

"What?"

"Those girls, the ones right behind us." I started to turn, but she whipped me forward again. "Don't look!"

"Okay," I chuckled.

"They don't think I can understand them."

"And?"

"They think you're adorable." She paused, listening again and almost laughed. "They'd like to see what's under your hood."

"Right," I said, shifting uncomfortably, pulling the hood farther over my head.

"They like your hands...and your ass."

"You're teasing me."

"I'm not!"

"What else do they think?"

She listened, her eyes shot open, her mouth widened. "I can tell you what *I* think. I think they want their faces punched." She began to turn around but I caught her, chuckling at her reaction.

"You're adorable, January."

She stood tall, turned toward them briefly then leaned into me.

"Sorry," she told me when I laughed at the not so subtle display. "I had to."

"It's okay, I kind of like you possessive." I leaned my face into the side of her hair and drank her in. "Can I ask you something?"

"Hmm?"

"Do you think I'm yours?"

"Yes," she said without hesitation.

"Good, 'cause I *know* you're mine."

She smiled at me. "Confident. I kinda like that."

I nodded.

"It's just not a conventional dating scenario, though, you know?" she said.

"Nothing about us is conventional, January."

"True," she said, but the smile on her face fell. "Oh shit."

"What?" I asked, following her line of sight. We watched Jonah walk through the front door. He waved sarcastically before breaking the threshold. "Damn it! How did he find us?"

"I don't know."

Inside, I searched the club for Jonah but he was nowhere to be found.

"He's got to be backstage," I said.

"He's a sneaky pete, dude."

"I know."

"What should we do?"

"They'll never believe we're also Seven reps. Not with Jonah back there."

"I could, you know, use my girlish wiles."

I looked at her, shocked. "I'm not going to pimp you out to gain backstage access, January."

"Why not?"

"Because that's disgusting!" I practically yelled, appalled.

She laughed at me. "Tom, it's not like I'm stripping or something equally sketchy. I was just going to flirt my way through."

"No," I said emphatically. I pulled her body to mine. "No way in hell. No."

I led us to the bar in the corner of the club.

"Fine, then what should we do?"

"We wait."

"And what if he talks to All the Pretty Girls before we get a chance? Dude, he is not above stealing. I told you this."

"I know. All we can do is play it by ear tonight, but from now on I'm not even telling Jason where we're going next. No one will know but us."

"Good idea."

"Speak of the devil," I told her as Jonah exited from the backstage entrance. I didn't have to bother getting his attention, he saw us.

"January," he said, wrapping his arms around her. I didn't care about appearances, I pulled him off her. I figured he'd misinterpret my possessiveness for anger at him for cheating.

"What the hell, Jonah?"

"What?"

"Don't play dumb, Jonah. How the hell did you know we were going to be here?"

Jonah laughed, clapping me on the shoulder harshly. I stared at this hand, a muscle ticked in my jaw. I shrugged his hand off roughly.

"I'm not joking with you, Jonah. How did you know?"

"Is Paris this secretive town no one knows about? I'm here for the music just like you."

"That's bullshit and you know it."

He smiled and shrugged his shoulders.

"Who are you stealing from us?"

"You're paranoid."

"No, I'm not an idiot. Who?"

"Not that it's not any of your business, but I just convinced All the Pretty Girls to visit Jason next week."

"Son of a-"

"Come on, Tom," January said, tugging at my arm to get me away from Jonah. "We'll still win," she whispered to me.

"January, feel like dancing?" Jonah asked as we started to walk away. January's hand tensed on my arm.

"No, thank you, Jonah. I'm busy working," she politely answered.

"Working. Is that what they call it now?"

We both turned around and I read the recognition in his face. He knew we were "together."

"What the hell does that mean?" I asked him.

"Nothing, see you next week."

"No, you won't," I told him.

"Oh, you will."

"And how would that be possible, Jonah? Unless you were cheating," I asked him, inches from his face.

January was grappling at my arm. "He's not worth it, Tom!" She yelled over the din of the crowd.

Jonah stepped closer. "Because you're going to tell me where you're going."

I laughed loudly and stepped back. "It'll be a cold

day in hell before I help your ass out. Do your own homework."

I turned to walk away but Jonah stopped me with his next sentence.

"You'll do it, or I'll tell everyone that you and January are sleeping together and that's the reason she's on the road with you."

January's grip on my arm tightened. "You wouldn't, Jonah." She spoke before I could.

"I would," he told her, a pathetic sympathetic expression on his face.

January's face looked amazingly hurt, making me want to pummel Jonah. "Why?" she asked him simply.

"It's business, January, nothing more." He smiled at her sincerely. *Asshole.* "I see how he looks at you. You're his only weakness. I've tried for years to one up this guy, but he keeps taking all the glory and for a while there I figured it was a lost cause trying to hit him where it hurts because nothing seemed important to this asshole. That is, until he met you."

Gently, I removed January's hands from around my bicep. I rushed Jonah in an instant, pinning him to the bar behind him. Several people scattered at once. "You tell a single soul that lie and I will make you hurt so bad, you'll wish you'd never been born." He started to laugh and I squeezed my hold around his neck even tighter, choking it off. "Do we understand one another?" I asked.

He nodded and I dropped him. He gripped the bar top, still grinning, casually resting against it as if I hadn't just threatened him. "Doesn't matter. I'll still find you."

"You won't."

"I will," he promised.

I guided a sullen January toward the exit. We couldn't get out of there fast enough. If I'd stayed another second, I would have wiped the floor with Jonah.

"We're leaving?" she asked me, dazed.

"Yes."

"What for?"

"He stole the band we'd come here to talk to but mostly because I can't be in the same building as that unethical bastard."

She nodded.

After a few minutes of walking the streets of Paris, we'd chosen to forget all about Jonah, purposely becoming absorbed in the beauty of the city.

Then it dawned on me. Watching January react to the city around her, I realized she'd never been here before.

"How is it possible?" I asked her.

She furrowed her eyes at me. "What do you mean?"

"This is your first time here, isn't it," I stated.

She blushed prettily. "It is."

"Oh my God and we're only here for another day. That's it. Come on, " I told her and yanked her toward the obvious.

"Where are we going?" she asked me.

"We're getting the Eiffel Tower out of the way, then we're going to see the real Paris tomorrow. The parts the tourists never see and you're going to speak to the locals and I'm going to watch your mouth as you do it."

"Je t'apprécie vraiment. Tu m'apprécies?" She surprised me, bringing me to a full stop.

I hugged her body closely and raptly watched her mouth. "Again."

"Je t'apprécie vraiment. Tu m'apprécies?" She repeated.

"What does it mean?" I asked her, swallowing hard.

"I told you that I cared for you and asked if you cared for me as well," she murmured softly.

"I do," I said without hesitation. I ran my hand across her forehead and down her face. "Speak to me again."

"What would you like me to say?" she asked.

"Whatever comes to mind."

She studied my face, then took a moment. "Tu es élégant. Tu me fascines. Te me rends heureuse. Je t'adore. J'ai besoin de toi. Je pense toujours à toi. Embrasses-moi."

I swallowed hard at how sexy I found her words and to my utter disbelief I'd had no idea what she'd said but they affected me nonetheless. "Tell me."

"Kiss me," she whispered.

I claimed her mouth harshly, breathing her in and tasting her tongue with my own before breaking away.

"All those words and all you asked me to do was kiss you?"

"There was more, but after that kiss I can't remember what I'd said."

"God, I wish I spoke French."

"You kiss with quite the French accent." *Zap.*

I kissed her again.

"You know, we could just go back to my room and I could watch you speak just as easily there," I taunted.

"You play to win, Eriksson."

"I know," I told her, smacking her cheek with a loud kiss. "We better stay out in public now that I think about it."

"Okay," she said, taking my hand. "Lead the way."

The Eiffel Tower was closed as it was so late in the evening so we stood underneath its belly, drinking in the cool metal and the intricately beautiful architecture. It truly was magnificent, I don't care what anyone says. Yeah, it may not have been the "cool" thing to do in Paris, but it most definitely was worth it to see. The structure was daunting and harsh but was so incredible in its artistry; it fit in so well with the nature around it. It was breathtaking...but not as breathtaking as the girl I was sharing its beauty with.

"I know where I want to go next," she told me.

"Tonight?"

"Yes."

"Where?" I asked, not caring about the time.

"We'll have to cab it. I think it's far from here."

"Where?" I asked again.

"Cimetière du Père-Lachaise."

"And what is the Père-Lachaise?" I asked, butchering the pronunciation. A chuckle built in her throat.

"You'll see," she explained, hailing a taxi.

She told the cabbie where to go in French and that earned her a place even closer to my side. Twenty minutes later, we'd arrived.

"It's a cemetery," I said gazing out the window.

"That it is, but not just *any* cemetery. This cemetery has a few famous bodies resting inside."

"Who?"

"Oscar Wilde, Edith Piaf, Jim Morrison. And that's just who I can remember off the top of my head."

"That's pretty cool, but how are we possibly going to see anything?" I asked, paying the driver.

"I always carry a flashlight in my bag."

"Why am I not surprised by this?"

"Got me. First stop? Oscar Wilde!"

"Why?"

"Because it's the only one I know how to find."

"This is rather adventurous for us. Cemetery. Night." I accidentally kicked a pebble beneath my shoe and January jumped. "Sounds."

"I think it's romantic," she said, squeezing herself into my side.

"That too," I agreed, kissing the top of her head.

The tomb was fairly near the side entrance we snuck through and it was...odd. I'm not kidding. It looked nothing like I thought it would. A seemingly solid slab, the side had a simple winged sphinx or maybe angel, depending on how you looked at it, carved into its side. It was shockingly contemporary in look and feel. Personally, I didn't like it, not for Wilde anyway. I mean, it was an unbelievably beautiful piece of art but for someone who lived and spoke aesthetics, it was too plain.

"Why is it barricaded?" I asked, running my palm up the glass fence surrounding the tomb.

"I kind of remember reading something about women kissing the sides of the tomb to the point it was deteriorating."

"Get out."

"I'm serious. We women can be a bit zealous at times."

"Is that so?" I teased, tucking her in to me as we perused the cobblestone paths along the tombs.

"If you think that's bad, you should hear the story behind Victor Noir's grave."

"And what's that?"

"Single women are supposed to kiss his bronzed face, place a flower in his upturned hat, and then proceed to fondle him in his most private of areas."

I laughed so hard, I startled her.

"No kidding and what does this get these single women?"

She cleared her throat. "A husband...in a year."

She got exceedingly quiet in that moment and I swear I could *feel* her blush.

I couldn't tease her for the myth—it didn't seem appropriate at the time, I didn't really know why. All I did know was that I didn't want to taint what could possibly be one of the most insightfully unintentional conversations I'd ever had. I shocked myself with that thought. January and I had...potential. A slow tingle permeated my stomach.

We walked a long time in silence, ducking behind trees and tombs when we suspected a guard may be approaching. We passed many graves but had no idea who they belonged to, if they were artists of any sort, be they writers, composers, painters.

We stumbled upon Jim Morrison's grave by accident. The only indication the tomb belonged to anyone of importance was the aluminum barricade cordoning it off. I couldn't believe how plain it looked as well. Though, the piles of flowers, candles and oddly, pharmaceuticals, were a sight to be seen.

"Thanks for *Light My Fire*, Jim," I told him. Although he was an exceedingly talented musician and for that I appreciated him immensely, I didn't personally care for the guy that much. I read once that he read heavily of existentialism. I'm a proponent of existentialism, but the Kierkegaard version and I tread carefully over those philosophies, especially Nietzche's. His version, one I'm assuming Jim followed, based on his actions, is nothing but dribble in my opinion, created to justify the whims of immoral behavior. And it was probably the reason Morrison felt the need to experiment with the drugs that eventually took his life. He was looking for fulfillment through "oneself" so he chose a material source like heroin, and as we all know fulfillment doesn't come that way. I know, I know, deep, right?

Not just a pretty face, ladies. Plus, unfortunately, I have a lot of experience in trying to "fulfill oneself." I just ended up unhappy in the end.

A little farther down and to the right, we spotted a brilliant white tomb with a woman draped and weeping over a broken lyre. Many of the tombs belonging to musicians were fashioned with broken instruments, a fitting tribute to their genius, I think.

"It's Chopin's," January told me, running her fingers along the wrought-iron fence surrounding the tomb.

"How fitting that the last grave we see tonight was the poet of pianists," I told her.

"How is that fitting?" she asked me honestly.

"Uh, maybe because *you're* a poet pianist?"

"Oh, hush."

"January, I'm not buttering you up. I'll get what I want from you regardless the compliment," I teased. She feigned dismay and made a move to hit me but I caught her hand, bringing her close. I whispered, "I'm telling you that you *are* a poet pianist. You have a lot in common with him."

She stared at me a long while and I let her. "I think that is probably *the* sexiest compliment I've ever gotten and if we were alone, I'd probably jump your bones right now."

"You tease." I smiled but looked around me. "January, there's no one here."

"Excuse him, Fred." She told the tomb and made an exaggerated movement with her head toward Chopin's grave.

"Oh, I apologize." We heard a noise and January literally jumped on me. "You're good on your word, MacLochlainn."

"Let's get out of here?"

"Yeah."

We walked toward the massive main double door entrance of the cemetery but discovered it was barricaded for the night.

"Crap, we're going to have to walk to one of the side entrances."

"Oh my God, that is, like, totally far away," January whined.

"Like, for sure."

"Shut up, Eriksson. It's one in the morning and we're illegally trespassing on a city cemetery. I'm a little nervous. I channel my inner Valley girl when I get nervous. I can't be arrested in every country we visit." She was quiet for a moment as we trekked it back and to the right. "Wait, is that something I should aspire to?"

"No, collect shot glasses or snow globes or something equally garish." I took her flashlight and turned the light off. The moonlight lit the cobblestone path enough to see where we were going. No sense creating a beacon for the guards. "If you can decipher which European country has the most comfortable handcuffs, I believe your goody two-shoes reputation may tarnish."

"Both of my shoes *are* very good." God, I found her unbelievably adorable when she said things like that. "But I already collect snow globes, remember?"

"Oh, yeah. Then collected arrests are the next natural step."

"Naturally."

"Naturally."

"You know who else is buried in here?" she asked.

"Who?"

"Abelard and Heloise."

"Seriously?"

"Don't make fun, Tom."

"What? I'm not. I'm seriously not. You know of

Abelard and Heloise?"

"Uh, yeah, I-I'm a bit of a history buff, if you couldn't already tell."

"January, it's like you were made for me," I told her. I realized what I'd said way late in the moment and the silence was palpable. The cemetery trip was proving to be way more discerning an occasion then I ever thought possible. It seemed that light was being shed even as we walked through the dark night. I shook it away. "You know what they say about history," I said, pretending I hadn't made things awkward or revealingly uncomfortable for myself.

"It's doomed to repeat itself?"

"I hope not," I said, shivering at the thought of Abelard's fate.

"You're thinking about Abelard, aren't you?

"Exactly."

"Let's change the subject then."

Chapter Nine

When the Levee Breaks

Thomas

"Have you ever been to Rome?" January asked me the next morning as she exited her room.

I had to swallow before answering or she would have realized she'd tied my tongue. She was wearing a dress. *Zap*. A short one. *Zap, Zap.* And as dark blue as her eyes, making me want to keel over at her feet.

"Never," I told her as I grabbed her bag from her. "January?" I asked her, walking a bit ahead.

"Yes, dear?" I smiled to myself, refusing to look at her.

"You look lovely today."

"Thank you," she said, an answering smile hidden on her face as well. I could hear it. "So, who's in Rome?"

"A South African band named *The Great Remember.* I've been wanting to see them for some time now. I got wind of them through a mutual friend of Jason's and mine."

"Cool. What's their sound?"

"Kind of a cross between folk and rock. Chicks will dig 'em. They use a lot of unusual instruments in their recordings as well as live, a lot of acoustic stuff, a lot of sweet sounding melodies. For some reason they favor G major."

"That's my favorite key."

"You may like them then. I haven't seen them live yet though, looking forward to it."

"Do you have anything by them?"

"I do."

"All right then."

"Have your medicine?" I asked her.

"Aye, aye, Cap'n!" She saluted me as we stepped onto the elevator.

"Have-Have you thought any more on Kelly's wedding?" I stuttered like a blithering idiot and settling in as the doors closed.

She hesitated. "Honestly? I don't think it would be wise for me to go."

She shifted slightly and leaned against the wall closest to her.

"Can I ask why?" I asked, my stomach dropping to my feet.

"Because, Tom," she said as we both stepped off the elevator, "I don't like being used and that's what I think you're doing." She left me with my jaw hanging open and checked us out of our rooms. All I could do was watch her beautiful figure and restrain myself from groveling at her feet, begging her to change the way she thought about me. I felt like such a pathetic loser. She had more control over me than I thought possible and I wanted so badly to feel bad about that but couldn't and that made me even more peeved. We cabbed it to the train station in a stony silence. I was fuming and could tell by her defiant body language that she'd caught on.

"Just out with it already, Tom."
We approached a bench to wait out our train.

"How in the hell did you get the impression I was using you?" I asked. She sighed loudly and plopped onto the seat. I sat next to her, closely. "How, January?" I whispered. There was more hurt in my voice than I'd imagined I'd allowed.

She turned her body so that her face was next to mine. "I won't be made a fool, Tom. Ever. I've had lots of practice at it and I'm confident enough to know that I'm worth more than showing up to a wedding on the arm of the man who's still in love with the bride."

I shook my head at her. "Haven't you been listening to me, January? I'm not in love with Kelly. I haven't been for more than six months. I'm completely and utterly over Kelly."

"Nobody gets over the love of his or her life in six months, Tom. Nobody."

I studied the stressed lines in her beautiful face and how the light glinted off her glassy blue eyes. I ran my fingers along the crease in her brow, relaxing the worry away.
And it clicked.

I let the recognition spread through the slow smile on my face and grabbed her shoulders, squeezing her into a hug, using every bit of restraint I had not to press too tightly. I wanted so badly for her to melt into me. "You're right," I secreted into her ear, crushing her to my chest. "Nobody gets over the love of their life in six months, January. Nobody. In fact," I told her, kissing her neck so softly it could have barely registered and speaking even softer. "You *never* get over the love of your life." I felt the movement of her neck as she swallowed my words. "I swear to everything, January, I am over Kelly."

I gently placed my mouth on hers and a surge of electricity seemed to pass between us. All I could think of was that I'd somehow zapped January MacLochlainn, that she'd been served a tablespoon of her own medicine and that its effects were immediate.

I'd fallen so hard in love with her, I was surprised I hadn't been knocked out cold.

And when I got to thinking about it, feeling so confident I was in love with Kelly Simsky six months prior was about the biggest joke I'd ever played...and it was on myself.

January

Oh. My. Lord. I'm in love with Thomas Eriksson.

Since our first kiss six months prior, I'd been falling hard for the stranger, but the short time I'd had him all to myself was enough to solidify it and in stone it seemed. I had it bad. It scared the crap out of me, to be perfectly honest. I'd only been in love twice before and both times I never felt it in my stomach the way I felt it with Thomas Eriksson. In fact, I was starting to question whether I truly loved the boys I thought I loved. They paled so white in comparison and further bolstered my confidence in my decision to wait. Tom was the only man, and I mean *man*, I'd ever met that could possibly endeavor to deserve my virginity and that made my insides tremble in cool anticipation.

I also wasn't prepared to experience the entire, almost exhausting, consuming sensation that was being in love with Tom. My body seemed to ache for him. My chest and stomach hurt a dull sort of pang whenever we were apart, even for a short time, and burst in a euphoric peace when he closed whatever gap lay between us, whether it be time or proximity. It was strange and exciting and altogether a feeling of extremes but, ugh, I wouldn't have had it any other way.

With my insane new awareness, I boarded the train headed for Rome with the most butterflies ever to take root in a person's stomach. I couldn't stop the stupid-ass smile on my face and I know my cheeks were glowing the deepest cherry they've ever shown but I was okay with that. I was so gosh dang cool with that it wasn't even funny. I wanted to do something terrible like run in circles on top of an Austrian mountain like Novice Maria in *The Sound of Music*, singing 'My love is alive for Thomas Eriksson!' I'd get my sisters to sing back up. Get the effing crackers out! Apparently, in-love-January is nothing but a ball of cheese. I was so high on what I felt for Tom, I could not care less what anyone thought of me.

Everyone, except for Tom, that is. I was pretty confident if I'd went around belting out my love for him in the key of ornery nun, he'd have me committed. It's why I was quiet instead and acting insanely unlike myself just staring at my folded hands. I looked over and found him smiling at me.

"What?" I asked, my cheeks burning deeper. *Maybe he'll think I'm embarrassed instead of cracked out of my noggin for him.*

"This," he said, running a finger over my blazing cheek, branding me with his equally hot touch. "You're so goddamned beautiful, January."

My eyes widened a bit at his heart felt exclamation. "Th-Thank you," I gulped.

"Come here," he said, leaning over my body. He enveloped me in his arms but didn't kiss me. He just *stared* and studied every line of my face. He looked at me with such unwavering intensity, he was stealing away my breath. My chest started pumping in air at an alarming rate. I was hyperventilating.

"Kiss me," I told him, never breaking eye contact.

"No," he said, his own warm, sweet breath wafting over my cheeks. His right hand moved achingly slowly from the small of my back and wrapped gingerly around my neck, resting his thumb at my rapidly beating pulse.

"Why?" I begged.

"Say it," he ordered, his eyes roaming mine.

I blinked long and slow, swallowing my fear. He knew. "You say it."

"Okay," he breathed but he was silent for what seemed like minutes.

"Please, I'm in misery, Tom."

"I'm trying."

"It's not hard."

He swallowed and the movement sent my eyes lazily down his neck and back up. "You'll reject me," he said when my eyes met his again.

"And so what if I do? Should it matter?"

He sank a little into himself then but I pulled him back against me.

"It shouldn't matter but it does," he told me.

"Don't."

"I can't-I can't be hurt again, January," he rushed out quietly in one breath. "There'd be no recovering, I told you that."

My heart pounded in my chest at the intended proclamation. "Say it," I ordered.

"I'm in love with you."

He said it simply, no hesitation between my last

asking him and that moment. Just five words between the old us and the new us.

He didn't wait for me to say it back. He rushed and kissed me *so hard* and yet not hard enough so I met him with equal fierceness. It was double the impact and exponentially delirious. So many wondrous sensations were assaulting me. His tongue sent tingles down my chin as it slid into mine. His goatee scratched softly against my cheeks, his hands held my jaw and threaded through my hair. I couldn't get close enough. I wanted so badly to climb into his lap. The very vague awareness I was in public held me back but barely. He pressed into me and we smashed against the window on our row. He was so warm and perfect, my hands went to his exposed t-shirt and my fingers laced within the fabric. I wanted to drag him over me but the tiny, almost infinitesimal rational side of my brain reminded me where I was.

A little kid giggling at us broke the spell. Tom's lips stilled on mine but their quivering told me they'd rather do anything but. My hands went softly to his face before fastening in his hair, running the length through my fingers until they met his neck.

I kissed him softly on the mouth and breathed my own revelation. "I'm in love with you, Tom."

He closed his eyes and let out a shaky breath before they shot open and held me in my place. "*Rome.*"

"What about Rome?"

"Just, promise me that while in Rome, you'll still feel the same way."

I sat up and rested my hand over his heart. "I promise." *You don't get over the love of your life, Tom. You said it yourself.*

He smiled the most heart-shattering smile.

He kissed my neck and I could feel him smile against my skin. "January MacLochlainn, how in the world did I get so lucky?"

I hugged him tightly. "Funny, I was just thinking the same thing about finding you."

I've never seen a more beautiful city than Rome, Italy. It was definitely a city of God. The architecture, the sheer number of churches, a city of art. That's what it was, a city full of art. Not one inch within its walls was untouched by a magnificent artist it seemed.

"It's incredible," Tom said, grabbing my hand after we completed a traditional coin toss into the Trevi Fountain, superstitiously ensuring a return trip to Rome. We saved the fountain for last since our hotel was right down the street.

We'd already visited Vatican City, numerous churches and many monuments. We weren't set to see The Great Remember until the following night. We thought about partying it up a little but, to be honest, we were worn out from the traveling and always being "on." We agreed to sleep in a little the next day as we rarely got to but not too late as we wanted to sightsee a little more.

"I want to take you on a proper date."

"*Really?*"

"Yes. American style. Dinner. Movie. Make out session."

"I'm down, Bobby Brown. What shall we eat?"

"Italian?"

"Very funny. And the film?"

"See, this is good. I think it's against an in-love law or something that we don't know what movies each other digs."

"All right, hold on?"

He nodded.

I found a man walking by and approached him. "Mi scusi, dove trovo un cinema?"

"A due isolati sulla destra"

"Grazie," I told the man.

He nodded and walked away with a polite, "Prego."

An inadvertent yelp came from me as I was swept off my feet and spun around. "You make me hot when you do that," Tom spoke into my ear.

I kissed him softly as he set me on my feet again. "Sei il grande amore della mia vita," I whispered into his lips.

He kissed me deeper. "And what does that mean?"

"Nothing. Come on, it's two blocks down."

As we walked to the theater, I started singing a Georgia Asher song we heard days before but stuck with us and to my utter surprise, Tom joined in harmony and we sounded unbelievably good together. His voice was rich and deep and perfect for harmony, which made sense to me knowing he played bass for The Ivories. When we were done, I looked over at him in awe.

"God you're talented, Tom."

"I am not."

"Yes, you *really* are."

"Yeah, yeah."

"I'm serious, Tom. You are talented as shit."

"This coming from one of the best pianists I've ever seen live." He paused. "Actually, that does kinda make me feel like a hoss, coming from *you*. Thank you."

"You're welcome," I said, blushing from his compliment.

The theater looked more like a ballroom than a movie cinema but that was Rome for you. I translated all the titles for him. It seemed they played oldies but goodies, and we had a choice between *Alien, Back to the Future, Indiana Jones: The Temple of Doom*, and three Italian flicks. Seeming as I would be the only one who could understand the Italian films, we opted for the American/Italian subtitled.

"So which one?" I asked.

"Of those three, I know exactly which one I'd pick, hands down, but I want to know if you'd pick the same one."

"I'd pick-," I began but he cut me off with a warm finger to my lips.

"No, let's play a game."

"Oooh, a game. I rock at games. I dominate at games. I am a game master."

"Are you finished?"

"Yes, proceed."

"Here's my card."

"Okay," I said, taking the little plastic Visa.

"I'll stand here while you buy your ticket. You go on inside, then it'll be my turn."

"And?"

"Hopefully we pick the same film."

"This game sucks," I told him.

"Just play along, January."

"Fine," I said, convinced he was going to choose *Alien* or *Indiana Jones.*

I debated whether I should just choose whatever film I thought he would want but that was defeating the spirit of the "game."

"Un biglietto per Ritorno al Futuro, per favore?" The attendant took the card, ran it and I pocketed my ticket.

"Your card, sir."

He took the card and palmed it in his hand.

"Thank you."

"I'll see you inside, then?" I asked, feeling unsure for some reason.

"In just a few. Need anything?"

"No, I can wait until later."

"All right," he said, leaning in and kissing my cheek.

Thomas

As soon as January went inside, I went to the attendant's window and purchased a ticket to *Back to the Future* hoping she chose the same one. I slid my card and the ticket inside my wallet. I took a deep breath and let it out slowly.

"Following us?" I asked Jonah casually as I turned to my left.

He hefted himself off the wall a few yards from the ticket booth, unfolding his arms and taking his sweet ass time to reach me.

"No. Just a coincidence."

"Right. A coincidence. You know what else might be coincidental?"

"What's that?" he asked, a dumb smile on his face.

"My fist connecting with your weak ass jaw."

"Tsk, tsk, Eriksson. Threats? Really? Don't make me report you to corporate."

"You're such a pussy when you say things like that. You know that?"

His only reply was a snort.

"Gonna run off and tell on me, Jonah? Can't fight like a man?"

"I'm a lover not a fighter, Tom. You know that," he said, a sarcastic tap on my jaw with his palm.

I gritted my jaw and pulled away from his reach. "Only cowards say shit like that."

"You always resort to violence, Tom. It's going to bite you in the ass one day, I think."

"I'm just not afraid to fight for what I believe in, but you obviously don't believe in shit seeming as how you're such a spineless, dishonest asshole. Not that you'd believe me, but I've never hit anyone in my life, yet I'm not afraid to start with you, dick. Get the fuck away from me before I'm good on my word."

I started to walk away but he grabbed the back of my t-shirt.

"Let go, Jonah," I told the air in front of me, refusing to face him. "I promise you, you won't win."

"Don't you want to know how I found you?" he asked, releasing his grip.

I hated that I did. I sincerely needed to know how the hell he was finding us since we told no one we were even going to Italy.

"How?" I asked, still refusing to turn.

"Why don't you ask January that question," he said, chuckling. My blood boiled to an intense heat, but when I turned to confront him he'd vanished around the corner like a slithering snake.

"What a crock of shit," I mumbled to myself. "She'd never betray me."

But he'd planted a seed in that moment and as much as I hated it, it made me think.

How did *he find us?* If January and I were the only ones to know where we were going and I didn't tell him, that left only one other person who could inform him. *Surely not,* I thought, shaking my head. *He's just trying to get inside your head.*

I entered the theater trembling from the need to hit something. I booked it to the attendant tearing tickets and handed over mine. He pointed to a theater to my right and said something in Italian I didn't understand. I just nodded and told him the only Italian word I knew. I hoped to God it was thank you but I couldn't be sure.

The theater wasn't yet dark and there was no one else inside but January. "Good, the previews haven't started," I told her, pasting the best smile I could attempt.

"Over here!" January shouted. She'd stood and started waving her arms. "I'm over here, Tom! Can you see me?" She joked. I looked on her. *There's no way she'd do that to you.*

"Yes, I can, January, seeing as we're the only two people in here," I joshed back, the lump in my throat only getting bigger.

"Oh good. I was afraid you wouldn't be able to find me."

"Your jumping up and down helped."

We settled into our seats and she rested her head on my shoulder. I swallowed my fear and tried to control my shaking.

"This isn't the film you bought the ticket for," she accused quietly.

"Yes, it is," I said, turning to meet her face.

"Then what took you so long?"

"Nothing, I just got a bit lost. I don't speak the language, remember?"

"You're lying," she said matter-of-factly.

"I am not," I said, lying through my teeth. "Here," I said, removing my ticket.

She took it and studied it, confirming what I'd already told her. "Hmm," she teased. "You pass, Christopher Lloyd, but something's still wrong, I can tell."

"Okay, Huey Lewis, I swear there's no news."

"You forget, I've got 'the power of love.'"

"It's a curious thing," I added dryly.

"Yeah," she said, "It's tougher than diamonds, rich like cream."

"Stronger and harder than a bad girl's dream," I continued.

"Oh my God, I don't know what's scarier, the fact we know these lyrics or the lyrics themselves."

"But it might just save your life, January. That's the power of love."

"Oh my God, I love you," she proclaimed.

I swallowed the lump away. "I love you too," I told her, kissing the top of her head.

And just like that, Jonah and what he'd told me melted away.

After dinner and the movie, I kissed her at her door and barely controlled my feet as they apparently had their own thoughts and began to make their way toward her bed with her in my arms. I abandoned her quickly, kissing her once more and sprinting to my own door. Inside my room, I dialed Harper, one of my best friends and Callum's wife.

"Yo, yo, yo!" I heard on the other line, making me smile.

"Harper Tate. What's new?" I asked her.

"Oh, besides the fact that it's seven in the morning here?"

"Oh, shit, sorry." I said, picking up the nearby alarm clock and trying to do the math. "I didn't think about that. I just needed to talk to someone."

"It's all right, buttercup. It's been over a week since you called. We were getting worried so it's all good. Why?" She sounded concerned. "What's wrong? Is it Kelly's wedding again?" Callum and Harper were the only ones who knew about my little Kelly issue. I heard a mumbling then Harper's muffled response.

"No, it's cool. It's Tom. I think he's depressed again about Kelly."

I rolled my eyes. "Harper, please tell Callum that I am not depressed about Kelly. I told you, I am so over Kelly it's not even funny. She's a friend and nothing more."

"All right, then what's up, man?"

"I'm, uh-" I cleared my throat. "I'm, uh,-"

"T-t-t-today, junior!"

"Shut it, Harper." I took a deep breath and just spit it out. "I'm in love." There was a long pause. "Harper?"

"Oh my God, with the girl? January?"

"Yes. But I know what you're thinking and this isn't Kelly-love, Harper. This is-this is...*it*."

"And you know this for sure?"

"I'd bet my life on it."

"I'd say that's pretty damn sure."

"It is."

"So what the hell is the problem then?"

"I'm having some trust issues, it seems."

"You sound like a chick, Tom."

"Christ, I know. It's embarrassing as hell."

"Well, grow a pair, dude. Suck it up. Because Kelly really didn't wrong you, you wronged yourself. If you're insecure, it's because you made yourself that way and there's no reason you should tiptoe around yourself because you're the toughest bastard I know."

"Damn, Harper, that was harsh."

"Well, I'm sorry. You needed to hear the truth and I love you too much not to be honest with you."

"Thank you for that, truly."

"Of course." I could hear her run and bounce on their sofa, then I heard Callum yell at her to stop throwing herself on the couch because it was scuffing the wall, then I heard her smile and roll her eyes.

Okay, I didn't *hear* that, but I definitely knew her well enough to know that it's exactly what she did. "You're not my dad, Callum," I heard her say.

"That's not what you said last night," I faintly caught.

"I'm outta here," I told her.

"Don't! Stay! Hold on! Do you say that shit to embarrass me?" she asked him.

"Yes," Callum answered as laughter faded away.

"Anyway. Tell me. What's she like?" she asked, the giddiness returning to her voice. Girls ate this crap up.

"I told you. Gorgeous, cool."

"Oh my word, boys are dumb. I'm gonna have to pry every detail from you aren't I? How tall is she?"

"I don't know, five-foot ten?" *She's exactly five-foot ten.*

"Her hair?"

"Long and brown." *The red highlights in it shine in the sun and all I want to do is bury my nose in it when she's around because it smells like cherry bark.*

"And her eyes?"

"Blue." *Like the ocean, blue.*

"She's a scout and your her apprentice so she must have killer taste in music. What else is she like?"

"She plays the piano like an absolute boss."

"No shit. That's cool. And her family?"

"She's the oldest of ten kids."

"*What*? That is wicked awesome. Her house must have been a riot to live in! Hey, I just thought of something, if she's *January*, then..."

"Yes, their names are the months of the year."

"Get the truck out of here! I may have to steal that idea. Callum, did you hear that! We're going to have to bear twelve children but no more than twelve!"

"I doubt Callum will agree to that, Harper."

"Oh, Tom," she laughed, "you know so little of my powers of persuasion."

"I guess not," I said, smiling at myself. "All right, it's late and I need rest to sightsee tomorrow."

"Crap. I'm so jealous of you. Have a good time but not *too good* a time, if you know what I mean."

"You're such a dork."

"Love you too, Tom. Talk to you later?"

"Yeah, tell Callum I'll talk to him next time."

"Okay. Bye, babe!"

"Bye."

I hung up the phone feeling a lot better about my stupid self-inflicted insecurities. Harper was right, they were pointless. I needed to get over it. I also couldn't wait for Harper to meet January. I had a feeling they would hit it off immediately.

A knock on the door broke me from my thoughts. I thought it might have been our laundry because I informed the staff that they could bring it by whenever it was done, regardless the time of night. I knew how the laundry services worked and since we usually needed to leave early the day after scouts, I always encouraged a "drop off when ready" policy. I opened the door but it wasn't the stodgy staff member I paid a twenty to have our laundry ready as soon as possible. Nope, it was freaking January MacLochlainn. In a t-shirt. And nothing else.

"Quick, let me in before someone sees me."

"Jesus, January, I can't have you in here looking like that." I tossed the door open and made way for her anyway because I wasn't an idiot. It was January MacLochlainn. In a t-shirt. And nothing else. I deserved at least a gander.

"I can't sleep."

"You definitely can't sleep in here." I gulped. "Not

looking like that, you can't."

"Why not?" she asked, worrying her bottom lip.

"Stop that."

"Stop what?"

"Worrying your lip like that. Just, stop."

"Okay," she said a bit hurt.

I growled. Yes, *growled* as my eyes traveled her length. "Yup, just as I imagined."

"I am?"

"Yes, and you damn well know it. Come on, I'm taking you to your room."

"Fine." She acquiesced easier than I thought she would but that was good news for me as I didn't think I could have survived another minute.

When we reached her door, I waited.

She patted her t-shirt clad body. "Oops."

I smiled and shook my head. "You did that on purpose, you clever minx."

She opened her mouth as if appalled then lost the expression and shrugged.

"I suppose I should go downstairs and get you another key?"

"No need. I can sleep in your bed...with you."

I ran my fingers harshly through my hair and blew a breath out quickly through my nose. "You are going to flipping kill me, January."

"It'd be a pretty sweet way to go, don't you think?"

"Don't say things like that," I told her, distancing myself a bit and shaking my head back and forth. "Now, what was I doing?"

"We were going to your room to lay down."

"Yes, that's what-No! No, I was going to get you a key. Yes, a key."

"Tom," she whispered, inching closer to me. She angled her face up at mine, our lips inches apart. "Let me sleep with you."

I blinked slowly, trying to gain composure. My heart beat rapidly and my chest pumped air desperately. "Let's-I don't think I can handle myself around you."

"Yes, you can," she teased, pressing a light, barely there kiss to my lips. A hand involuntarily palmed her ass as I pressed her into me and kissed her deeply.

"No, I can't," I said, pulling away quickly. "Did all the air just...*leave*?" I asked the stifling hall around me.

"Come on. Come with me," she tempted.

I followed her like a lost puppy back into my room. "It's your funeral, kid."

She shut the door behind us and pressed me against its back. "Does this feel familiar?"

I switched places with her lightning fast, making her giggle. "Now it does."

I kissed her again but this time slowly, languidly, biding my time, memorizing every curve, every line of her lower and upper lip. And I continued to kiss her until I found us laid down on the bed, her legs wrapped around my torso.

I sat up and shoved myself off. "Get under the covers, January."

"What?" she asked, surprised.

"Get under those effing covers, right now."

"Okay," she said, confused.

I paced the room a bit, pulling my t-shirt over my head as I thought quickly about my plan. I made the mistake of peering her direction. She looked like she could eat me whole. "Don't." I laughed hysterically. "Just don't, January."

"I'm sorry," she said as her attractive blush painted across her cheeks.

"Oh, God!" I said, panicked. I ran my hands through my hair over and over. "I'm a glutton for punishment! I'm a masochist! You've made me a masochist, J! I've been a lot of things but never a masochist."

"You are not a masochist, dorkwad."

"I am! I am because I'd rather suffer through this night and every night after with you by my side, so unbelievably attractive and so sexy as hell, and not be able to do anything than *not* have you here. That's masochism, January."

She sat up a little, her t-shirt pooling around her thighs. I had to look away. "And who said we couldn't do anything?"

"Me."

"Why?"

"Because you're a freaking virgin, January."

"So?"

"Listen, you don't just give that shit away especially to guys like me."

"I happen to think you're a pretty neat guy. Oh, yeah, and there's the little fact that I'm in love with you."

Those words soothed my aching, edgy soul and my breathing instantly steadied. "I love you too," I told her.

"Then come here. I have something to give you."

"No, I can't, January. I can't."

"You don't want it?" she asked, the hurt outlining her entire face.

I fell on the bed beside her. "January, I want it, probably more than I've wanted anything in my entire life but not like this."

"Then how?" she asked softly, her hand reaching up to rest on my face.

I took her left hand with my right and looked down at it, thumbing her ring finger. Her gaze followed mine and she realized what I'd meant. She nodded slightly, smiled sweetly and we settled into bed.

She, wrapped in my arms, and I, wrapped around the third finger of that left hand.

Chapter Ten

The Song Remains the Same

Thomas

The next morning, after we woke and I got January back into her room, I went to tell her we should get going and accidentally caught the tail end of a telephone conversation. That wasn't all that bad and if I'd left as any normal person would have, giving her privacy, I'd probably be the happiest jackass this side of the Mississippi, but I didn't do that. No, in a typical asshole Thomas move, I stuck around to listen in. That was bad, for many, many reasons and a move I was going to pay dearly for. Believe me.

"We'll be in Stockholm tomorrow." I heard her say over the phone, making my heart race and my skin panic. *No, she's not. She's not.*

"Probably around three in the afternoon by the looks of it," she continued, then laughed. "No, he doesn't suspect a thing." My heart sank to my feet.

"No, don't even bother." *Don't bother?* "All right, love you too. Uh-huh. Tomorrow then."

That's when I discovered that I was a gullible bastard.

January

"We'll be in Stockholm tomorrow," I told my sister July.

"What time? So I know to tell Dad."

"Probably around three in the afternoon by the looks of it."

She paused. "Hey, has Tom figured out what a massive dork ass you are yet?"

"No, he doesn't suspect a thing," I teased, folding a scrap piece of paper in my lap.

I heard the front door open and close and knew it was my father returning home from work. He would expect his usual hourlong conversation if he found out I was on the phone, but I knew Tom was ready to leave soon. I reminded myself to call him later the next day.

"Do you have time to talk to Dad, actually? He just walked in," July asked.

"No, don't even bother."

"Okay, I love you, January. Be careful over there. Should I tell Dad tomorrow then?

"All right, love you too. Uh-huh. Tomorrow then."

Thomas

I should have told January that I saw Jonah the night before but I didn't. I don't know why I didn't. I guess I was still letting a small piece of my insecurity control the rational side of my brain when it came to that fact. Truthfully, I wanted to know how he was finding out where we were and as much as I hated to admit it, her phone call made my heart ache. I hated to jump to conclusions, but that's exactly what I was doing.

"I called The Great Remember up this morning," I told her stoically as we made our way to see them. "Did I tell you that?" I asked, studying her reaction.

"Oh? Well, that's a good idea, I suppose. What'd you say?" she asked, peering up into my face. She was so beautiful and innocent-looking. You're *reading too much into that call, Tom.*

"I just let them know our names, who we were, and that they could expect to see us after the show."

"You didn't tell them about Jonah?" she asked.

"No, should I have?"

"I don't think so. I was just wondering."

She grabbed my hand as we walked to the venue. Her thin fingers felt so cool to the touch, I absently brought them to my mouth and blew on them. *She wouldn't betray you.* I told myself. *You can't fake sincerity like that...But, maybe she's just playing you. Maybe she's Jonah's inside man...No fucking way!* I argued with myself. *January would never do that. She's not capable. I'd bet my life on it.*

"Hey," she said, breaking me from my thoughts. "What's got you so worried?"

I forced a smile. "Just thinking."

The Great Remember was phenomenal live, but I was so distracted with watching January then watching out for Jonah, I almost missed the potential.

"Shouldn't we, *you know*?" January asked me as I nursed my beer.

"Huh?"

"*Meet them*?"

"Oh shit. Yeah."

"What's up with you?"

"Nothing," I dodged. "Hey! Richard!" I said, catching the attention of the lead.

He looked up at us approaching and smiled.

"Hi, I'm Tom. This is January. We're from Seven. I spoke to you earlier on the phone."

"Oh, God. You really came," Richard said, a thick South African accent crowding his words. "Guys! Guys! This is Tom and January. They're from the label I told you about!"

The rest of the band clamored around us and we spent hours with them, they agreed to travel to Dublin from Rome to meet with Jason as he was coming to Europe a bit earlier before attending the Windmill Festival. The Great Remember were going to be huge. So, why didn't I feel any sense of triumph?

The next morning, I grabbed my duffel as well as January's.

"Good morning," January greeted me.

"'Mornin'."

"Oh! Oh, dear!" January suddenly exclaimed.

My head whipped around toward her. "What's wrong?" I asked, dropping our bags to the floor. My hands searched her body for injuries.

"Oh, it's just, I don't know how to tell you this..."

"What?" I asked, my heart beating wildly in my chest.

She eyed me carefully, with pity in her eyes. "Follow me, I need to show you something."

I picked our bags up and followed her into the room, prepared to hear her admit to everything, to hear she couldn't take the burden of the guilt. I sat at the edge of her bed after abandoning the bags on the floor. I looked up at her when the door clicked shut.

"What did you need to show me?" I asked solemnly.

"This," she whispered, taking my face in her hands and kissing me harshly.

And like a moth to a flame, I grabbed her and brought her to my body, bringing her on top of me as we laid back on her bed. I kissed her back like there wasn't going to be a tomorrow, like I wouldn't get the chance to kiss her like that again.

She stopped me and brought her face mere inches above mine. "'Tom," she said.

I closed my eyes briefly. "Yeah?"

"Whatever it is that's bothering you. Stop it. You'll get through it. *We'll* get through it."

She kissed me again and we made out like that for an hour. I could have done it all day with her. She did love me. She had to. It was in the way she breathed in my mouth when she kissed me, the way she grabbed my shoulders to get as close to me as possible, in the way she reassured me that we'd get through whatever was bothering me. She had no idea the magnitude of my troubles but she said "we'd get through it." There was no way she could betray me. She loved me. *She loves me,* I kept repeating to myself.

"I think we missed our train," she said behind closed eyes, still inching her way up my neck.

"I don't care," I told her. "We'll book another room here and go straight to the Windmill Festival tomorrow."

We laid like that the rest of the day talking and making me forget the telephone call...sort of.

Because seeds of doubt are one of those things. They fester and burrow and feed off uncertainties until they've grown into one massive tree of shades and shadows that hover over all you've known confidently as the truth. The leaves rustle and whisper in your ear all the everythings you wished to

God weren't true and they are unrepentant, determined to convince you that the doubt is out to get you. And although you scream, "Enough!" Ready to chop that damn tree down, they've somehow hidden your ax. It's nowhere to be found.

So the doubt swallowed me whole.

Paris was as we had left it. Beautiful as always, but this time there was a sheen of dishonesty associated, creating a foreboding feeling to permeate my skin. The more I thought about the phone call, the more I realized I couldn't have heard incorrectly, but maybe I *had* heard January being used. I thought her too honest, too naive to willingly screw me over. That was not January's style.

"Back to the hoodie, I see," January said, breaking me from my thoughts.

"Huh? Uh, yeah. It's still a little chilly out." I tugged the hood of my jacket farther over my face.

"Mmm, hmm," she hummed under her breath.

I wasn't taking the bait. "There's a couple of day bands, but I've screened them already and I'm not interested."

"So have I and I concur."

"I do want to see a band called Clever. Many of the labels are going to be interested in this one, but I know someone who knows someone who got them to see me first."

"Shut the eff up!"

"No."

"Jeez, chill, Tom. I was just joshing," she said, elbowing me softly.

"Sorry," I said absently.

"Where are they playing?"

"Reine."

"Ah, I see."

"This is a joint effort by several labels, January. There'll be media there."

"Media."

"Pic ops. I doubt we'll be put in any of the press, but Jason said we have to dress up anyway."

"What! I didn't bring anything!"

"Jason took care of that."

January

We reached our rooms at ten in the morning and I was only slightly freaking out that I could or could not be photographed and might or might not be put into print, immortalized forever as the slob who obviously dressed from a duffel bag for the largest music festival in Europe, but Tom assured me that Jason had that all figured out so I decided not to freak out...too much.

"Ready?" Tom asked me as I opened my door to him.

Tom had been acting very strangely, resorting to wearing his hood over his head again and I was slightly concerned at how ice-cold he'd been acting toward me, but I wasn't going to let this get to me. He would come to me and talk when he was ready.

"Yeah, where are we going?" I asked.

"Here," he said, handing me a note and a handful of cash before walking off.

I peered down at my hands. "Wait!" I said laughing. "Where are you going?"

"I've got some business to attend to."

"Some business to tend to," I mocked his deep voice. "Sorry little missus, this big man has things to do I wouldn't tax your tiny lady mind with. I got this."

He sighed and rolled his eyes. *Condescending jerk.* "It's nothing to do with the label, January. It's personal."

"Oh," I said. "All right, can I just come with you then?" I asked, grabbing his hand.

"No," he said, pulling away, wounding me. "Uh," he said, clearing his throat. "Listen, Jason's waiting for you."

"And I take it you don't need new threads then?"

"No, well, yes, but Jason's got my measurements. I trust him. I've gotta go. Have fun," he told me before taking off down the corridor.

I just stared after him, wondering what in the hell crawled up his butt. Then I *ogled* his rude butt and thought, "nice ass" but shook myself and remembered that he needed a swift kick there not an appreciative stare.

I went back inside, grabbed my purse and hailed a cab.

"Où aller?" the cabbie asked me.

I looked down at the paper in my hand and almost keeled over in happiness, recognizing the name of one of Paris' most elite and most gorgeous department stores, Galeries Lafayette.

Ten stories high, the store can be found on Boulevard Haussmann, and oh my Lord it is just unbelievably decadent. I couldn't wait to go there. Sometimes working for the label really paid off, but *sometimes... Le sigh*. Oh well.

Jason was outside the front doors smoking a cigarette when I pulled up. He reminded me of home. Seeing him, coupled with Tom's cold demeanor and missing my family like crazy, I unexpectedly burst into tears. I don't know why I did it. I just needed a friend in that moment it seemed, and it had been weeks since I'd seen a friendly face from home. I was overwhelmed, I suppose. That and I didn't know what was going on with Tom.

When Jason saw me he smiled but saw my tear-soaked face and threw down his cigarette. I ran to his arms and threw them around his neck.

"Oh, Jason," I wailed pathetically in his ear.

His chest shook with laughter. "Oh, January!" He teased.

"Shut up!" I said, pulling away while laughing and wiping away my tears.

Jason pulled me back to him and hugged me harder, making me sigh. "What's up with you, January MacLochlainn? Hmm? Why the sour face?" He ran his thumbs underneath my eyes.

"Oh, I'm just so happy to see you," I semi-lied.

"Oh, just happy to see me, is it? Could it be you're sick of Tom as well?"

"A little," I admitted not realizing how true that really was. I loved Tom so much, but I wasn't an imbecile. The way he'd been treating me these past two days was alarming to say the least.

"Come on," he said, wrapping his arm around my neck and swinging me toward the doors of the fanciest store I'd ever laid eyes on.

"We are going to stick out here like a sore thumb, Jason."

"Yeah, we might have one of those 'Pretty Woman' moments."

This made me laugh.

"Yeah," he said, spreading his free arm before us, "imagine it. They'll look down at you in disdain, perk their noses in the air and say with their haughty French accents, 'You are not Lafayette material, miss!' Then I'll step in and save the day by flashing my black card. They'll cower and bow at your feet, kissing your shoes and begging your forgiveness."

"You have quite an imagination, Jason."

"I know, I should have been a writer instead, but I've heard there's no money in it."

We stopped and took in the magnificence of the store. It felt like I was standing within a giant Fabergé egg. The word opulent came to mind, plenty of times.

"The world is your oyster," Jason said, kissing my temple, making me want to cry again, "and it seems you need it."

I wanted to call Tom and run to him, but I also wanted to ignore Tom or find him and slap him in the face. I was a dichotomy of feelings, but one thing was for sure, I needed to talk to him, to get it out there. If he was regretting being with me or telling me he loved me, then I needed to know, so I could get over it and move on. I had more respect for myself than to endure disrespect. I was a MacLochlainn, damn it!

We went to a few stores but nothing really stuck out at me. It was either too formal or too casual. Jason explained that the festival was usually a light affair, but the first night, if you're lucky enough to be invited, the labels throw a party at one club hosting several up-and-coming bands and it's usually a dressy night.

"I don't know about these stores, Jason. I'm not seeing anything."

"There's plenty to choose from. You're just obsessed with price tags. Stop. Just find something you'll look good in and put it on."

"How eloquently said."

"Well, I don't know shit about this kind of stuff. Listen, I'm gonna go find some digs for Tom. Find something then I'll come find you."

"All right," I sighed.

Perusing the stores was a lot of fun but Jason was

right, I was afraid of the price tags.

"If Seven doesn't care, neither do I," I bolstered myself.

I called the attention of a woman in a store full of couture, but she didn't shy away from me. In fact, she was extraordinarily kind and seemed excited to help me. She told me I was the perfect model for the clothes in her store, but somehow I doubted that. I told her to work her magic and an hour later, Jason found me with a few new things in hand, including a few *essentials* that I believe I would have rather died than buy in front of Jason but I had no choice.

"What is this, La Femme Nikita?" he asked, picking the lacy object up with one finger.

I shoved it all down back on the counter and knew the blush that burned my face would take days to calm down.

"Jason, I swear. Don't embarrass me."

"I'm sorry, kitten," he smiled. "Mwar!"

"Oh my God, you're never going to let me live this down."

"No, I'm not. In fact, I might just rub it in Tom's face."

"Why would that affect Tom?" I asked, prying. *Does Jason know*?

"Oh nothing," he dodged.

The woman wrapped my things and we walked out of there with one dress that probably cost more than my entire wardrobe. My mother would kill me if she knew.

Jason dropped me off at the hotel and when I reached my room, I dropped my things inside before knocking on Tom's door.

"Tom?" I asked the door as I rapped lightly with my knuckles but there was no answer.

I sighed in frustration, and thought it was probably a

good idea to take a nice long bath in my room's huge tub before I got ready for the evening.

I showered and shaved first, then soaked for at least an hour and almost fell asleep the water was so warm and the tub so deep. When I got out, I'd never been so clean. I rubbed the condensation away from the mirror and took a good long look.

"Right, you're a mess, January." That's when I realized. I had absolutely no curling iron or straightener or even a blow dryer to my name. I started to panic before remembering a salon downstairs. I rang Jason to ask him if I could charge a mani and pedi as well as a styling and he approved without thinking. I'm sure he had no idea how much it all would cost. I was positive I'd be fired over the whole thing but Jason was so blasé, I decided I could be as well.

I threw on a pair of yoga pants and a button-down and headed downstairs. In French, I told the lady I needed "the works" and she understood the American idiom. Maybe it was universal. I decided I didn't need to do anything too crazy with my hair and opted to leave it down and in large, loose curls. I have to admit I allowed them to go a bit insane with my makeup, especially on the eyes, but it was a night out and I didn't want to feel like my dreary usual self.

My dress was black, super short, and insanely sexy and the last thing I needed was for someone to whisper "it's too much." I thought the dress was still a bit over the top, in fact, but the sales girl assured me I looked great in it and it was just understated enough so I trusted her. I was doing that a lot, giving everyone carte blanche, but lately the check was proving bad. Hopefully, the girl hadn't steered me wrong.

When all was said and done, I had to admit I looked pretty damn hot. I walked away from the salon feeling like a brand-new woman, heading straight for an empty room probably down the hall from yet another presumably empty room belonging to the elusive Thomas Eriksson. I was tripping myself out. I felt bipolar. One minute I was high as a kite, the next, I was down in the dumps. *Don't let a guy make you feel like that, January, especially one who claims he loves you. Rise up, girl!* I decided I was going to have fun that night even if I had to beg Jason to be my date.

At nine o'clock that night I was ready, dress on, makeup, hair, and nails done. I stood in front of the mirror and did a double take at the reflection. I was staring at one sexy mama and I felt really damn good about that. I smiled at myself.

Knock! Knock!

I jumped at the sound at the door. *Time to pay the piper, Tom.* He was going to eat his actions if I had to stuff them down his throat with the painfully gorgeous heels strapped around my feet.

I flung the door open but my carefully constructed smile fell at my knees when I saw who it was.

"Jesus, January," Jonah told me, eyeing me up and down.

"What do you want, Jonah?"

"I'm here to escort you. Jason sent me."

"Jason sent you?" I asked, shocked.

"Yeah, apparently *Tom* is too busy to take you."

"You're lying."

"I'm not. Here," he said, offering me his cell phone. It was already ringing Jason.

"Yo!" I heard.

"Jason? Jonah is taking me to the club tonight?"

"Yeah," he said, clearing his throat uncomfortably. Something was up. "Uh, Tom is indisposed. He said he'll see you here."

I hung up. "That son of a..."

"What's that?" Jonah asked, a devious smile on his face.

"Shut up, Jonah. Let's go."

I grabbed my bag and stuck in a few essentials before letting the door click behind me.

"Good God, January," he began. "I gotta admit, you've got to be one of the sexiest women ever. You're making me think twice about my girl back home."

"Classy, Jonah."

"No shit. You are smoking hot. What would you say..."

"Stop!" I said, holding up my hand to get away from his slime. "I wouldn't mess with you if we were the last two people on Earth and our need to procreate was the difference between the continuation of the world or not. That's how much I hate you."

"So..."

"Absolutely not, Jonah. Take me to the club and leave me the hell alone."

"Feisty little thing."

"Ugh! You are beyond creepy."

When we reached downstairs, there was a car waiting for which I was eternally grateful. The club was only two blocks but I didn't think I could survive my heels much less Jonah's incessant come-ons.

We pulled up to the club and true to Tom's word, there were paparazzi, their cameras flashing at an astronomical rate. I was so freaking nervous, I could vomit. Jonah started to exit the cab but I pushed him back.

"Don't even think for a second you're exiting this car in front of me. You're going to let me leave, then you're going to circle the block so no one knows we rode together."

"Fine," Jonah admitted too easily, sitting back.

I stepped out of the car and shut the door behind me, ensuring Jonah wasn't following. The clicks of lights were blinding and took a moment to become accustomed to. I followed the walk in front of me slowly so as not to trip and made a beeline for the entrance but was stopped short just a few feet into the promotional backdrop. Photographers clambered my direction and insisted on a picture. *Fine,* I thought, *give them a picture to shut them up. They won't publish a nobody.*

I posed as best I could and moved but was stopped again...and again and again. Finally, I made it to the door and broke the threshold feeling part exhilarated, part terrified. Either way I was glad it was over.

Thomas

I sat just behind the door not expecting to see January for at least an hour. I wasn't keeping an eye out for her...All right, I was definitely keeping my eye out for her, but I was also doing my job, waiting for one band in particular that I recommended for tonight's performance and I was eager to talk with them. In other words, eager to get Jonah away from them.

That's when I saw her and literally lost my balance resting against the door. I scrambled for some semblance of cool but couldn't tear my eyes away.

"Oh Jesus," I heard behind me.

I turned to find Jason. "What?" I asked, knowing full well what he meant and who he meant it for.

"I had no idea."

"I did," I told him, staring after the most breathtakingly beautiful woman I'd ever seen in person and Christ was she a natural at it. She looked supremely uncomfortable, but I was willing to bet I was the only one who would have been able to tell that in the way she held her arms a little stiffer than usual.

"And you're in love with her," Jason said matter-of-factly.

"I am," I said without reservation, still staring at her.

"This time it's real," Jason said, folding his arms and leaning against the wall next to me.

"I know it is."

"Then why the hell have her come here alone?" he asked me.

"Because..." I offered, not really sure what to say.

"She's in love with you too," he said, trying to get my attention but I still was unable to tear my eyes away.

"No, she's not."

"The hell she's not," he told me. "I was with her all day and I know January. She's in love."

"Yeah, with Jonah," I said, not really knowing if that was true.

Jason laughed so loud it caught the attention of one of the security guards at the entrance. "That's rich," he said, sucking in a breath. "My God, you really are the world's biggest fool." He walked away, shaking his head, and muttering, "What an idiot."

January was approaching the end of the walkway so I sank into the shadows a bit and watched her break the threshold. She brought the backs of her hands to her flushed cheeks and smiled to herself, but her expression quickly turned to worry and what looked a little like determination. I never wanted to touch someone so badly as I did January in that moment. I fisted my hands at my side, bolstering myself with the memory of that phone call. I needed to talk to her about it but tonight was not the night. We had a job to do and it needed to be done before Jonah showed up. That R&D spot was mine.

Inside, the club was noisy and ridiculously crowded and I lost January pretty quickly but somehow found Jason again.

"Have you seen January since she's come in? I need her to be there when the band shows up."

"No, I haven't," he said, taking a swig of a dark liquid.

"I'll have to look around then. I might have to meet the band without her."

Jason was called to the bar for some kind of alcohol emergency and had to leave me to myself. I scanned the crowd below me and tried to see through the smoky, dark room. Intermittent laserlike lights would cascade over the heads of the club patrons and would highlight randomly, allowing me to see for short periods of time. My second sweep across the floor provided me a glimpse of her and my eyes strained to see through the fog so I inched closer and got the biggest surprise of my life.

January. *Hugging* Jonah.

My heart pounded severely against my ribs and my mouth went dry. I gripped the handle of the railing and leaned over as much as I could without falling to my death.

What a traitorous bitch, I thought to myself. My heart turned to mush inside my chest and for the first time in *years* I wanted to cry. *Well, if I wanted to know what it really felt like to lose the love of your life, the one person truly made for me, I've definitely gotten my fucking wish.* I scrubbed my hands over my face and through my hair. They were unsure what to do with themselves. *I've got a job for you*, I told my hands as they fisted into white knuckles. I pushed myself from the railing and booked it down the stairs into the belly of the beast. I'd lost sight of them through the undulating crowd so I pushed through without regard for the guests around me.

I broke through close enough to catch another glimpse of them but stopped cold when I saw she wasn't hugging Jonah, she was *shoving* Jonah, fighting his roaming hands and *crying*. The adrenaline hit me like an atomic bomb, realizing I was the biggest dumbass in the world. She wasn't the traitor, *I was.* I was so quick to think ill of her, afraid that I'd get hurt, that I was willing to jump to ridiculous conclusions, despite the fact that January hadn't ever done anything for me to distrust her so wholly.

I pushed harder and with new vigor. I needed to get to her. She needed me and I hadn't been there for her. My heart tore in two, aggravating an already ragged wound. I'd been the betrayer, not the betrayed. I felt sick to my stomach as I made my way through the thick group of people.

"Get off of me!" I heard her scream, tears streaming down her face. "Stop!"

"January!" I yelled but she couldn't hear me over the pounding bass. "January!" I tried again but it did no good.

I felt like I was making no progress. I was failing her. No one around her noticed her predicament except me and I was failing her. Her arms were red and swollen from his mishandling her and I couldn't fucking get to her!

Suddenly, I heard faint but gut-wrenching screams come from the direction of the DJ booth and everyone's heads whipped that direction.

"Feu!" I kept hearing, the panicky words screaming from invisible lips. I had no idea the meaning until I saw January's eyes had grown round in her head. She searched the crowd around her and her eyes fell on me.

"Fire!" She screamed at me.

No.

"January! Come to me!" I yelled at her as Jonah fled, cowardly leaving her there to fend for herself.

I reached my hands toward her and she extended her arms, desperation lacing her expression. We pushed and strained for one another, the tips of her right hand brushed mine and for the first time, I felt slightly relieved that she was close to my possession. I grabbed for her, but her grip escaped mine just when I thought I had her. *No*! I pushed and tossed people away from me but the panicked cloud of people clambering for the nearest exit seemed to swell in numbers and January was too light to fight back. Every time I made an advance, people would push her back.

"Help me!" She screamed, making my heart wrench.

"Move!" I hopelessly yelled at the people in front of me, but it did no good. My stomach dropped to my feet. January was swallowed whole and I was helpless to watch. I'd failed her. Completely.

Chapter Eleven

All the Pretty Girls

Thomas

I followed the direction I thought she was being pulled as black, billowing smoke engulfed the massive ceiling of the club. I had maybe a minute. People's piercing screams haunted my ears as I spun around feebly in frenzied haste.

"January!" I hysterically called out. My body was begging me to run, to act, to save, but I couldn't see her, fear locking up every ounce of common sense.

The crowd was thinning out and I breathed a slight sigh of relief, hoping I'd get to her. The smoke was becoming so thick and lower to the ground, I had to bring my shirt over my mouth. It didn't help much and I began to choke and cough as I inhaled the charred remains of the building burning down around me. The heat was becoming unbearable but I was determined to find her. I would have died before I left her in that club.

I frantically searched the people around me, gripping them as I went and ensuring they weren't January. I went from person to person until the black cut off my view and two hands reached for me.

"No!" I told the person dragging me toward what I assumed was some sort of exit. "No!" I exclaimed, pushing back but they succeeded in pushing me into the night air. I coughed and gagged as I reached soil and fresh air but immediately got back up, determined to find her.

The fireman who pulled me out, pushed me toward the crowd, unwilling to let me back in. "January!" I yelled at the building, begging her to come out.

I immediately turned toward the crowd surrounding the burning building and searched for her face. I hysterically wound my way through the throngs of stunned faces calling out her name.

"Tom!" I heard to my left and ran toward the voice.

"Jason!"

"Are you all right?" he asked. "Where's January?"

"I don't know! Help me find her!"

"I got out pretty early," he told me as we weaved our way back through the gathering. "I didn't see her come out, Tom." His own voice was struck with fear she hadn't come out.

"She's here," I told him confidently, desperately. "She has to be here." I was trying so hard to hold on to that. My blood began to run cold as we reached the edge of people with no sign of January. "She's here. She's here." I repeated over and over.

"Okay, okay," Jason said, pacing the outside of the crowd. "We must have missed her. We had to have."

My body began to shake in trepidation, in terror. I noticed a police cruiser nearby and ran to it. The back doors were open and I noticed a bullhorn sitting on the floorboard in front. I ran to the passenger's side and opened the door, grabbing the horn. My trembling hands fumbled with the on switch and I numbly tried to work the buttons. I leaped onto the hood of the car and peered over the crowd.

"January!" I yelled as everyone's shocked expressions turned my direction. "January MacLochlainn, are you there?!"

People began to search around themselves, searching for the name I'd just called out, but there was no answer and the dread began to run icy in my veins.

"January?" I asked them. "Please," I begged as horror slowly thread through my words. "January, please. Please, answer me."

But nothing.

My eyes searched rapidly but my body shuddered at the realization that she wasn't there. The bullhorn slipped from my fingers, tumbling to the cobblestone below. Women surrounding the car drank in my shaking body and knew what the silent response meant. Many of their hands went to their mouths, a recognition of my supposed loss. The sight of their conclusions made me want to vomit. I jumped from the hood and ran smack into Jason who stood there, drawing the same conclusion of those around me.

"She just couldn't hear me," I told him.

"Of course," he said, but his glassy eyes betrayed his words.

"Don't," I pleaded. "She's here. She's here."

"Tom," he said quietly, placing his hand on my shoulder.

"No!" I said, throwing it off, but my body shut down and I was forced to drop to my knees. "She's here. She's got to be. She's got to be."

An ambulance blew by and the hope that'd been dying in my chest roared back to life.

"The hospital," I told the ground.

"Come on," Jason said, dragging me to my feet.

We ran up the block and hailed a passing cab. Jason told the driver to take us to the nearest hospital using his pocket translator. I was relieved we were moving but no matter how fast we were moving, it still wasn't fast enough for me and I sat at the edge of my seat, hunched over the window, staring at the traffic ahead. My knee bounced at an ungodly pace.

I examined Jason's face quickly, noting that neither of us seemed to have inhaled any smoke. Our mouths and noses were clear of black unlike a few I saw back at the club. I thanked God for small favors.

"She's going to be there," Jason said, reassuring me.

"I know," I said, but not as confidently as I'd have liked.

I rubbed the palms of my hands together quickly and silently prayed that she would be there. We pulled up to the entrance of the hospital and jumped from the cab, leaving Jason to handle the transaction. I ran through the emergency doors and frantically searched the blackened faces of those who'd already arrived, but none of them matched my January's. My heart flipped in my chest.

I ran up to a nurse. "I'm sorry. Do you speak English?"

She gave me a sympathetic smile and searched around the desk around her, finding a girl sitting at a desk nearby. She grabbed the girl's sleeve and said something in French. The girl jumped up and took in my sooty clothing.

"Yes? I speak English."

"Oh, thank God! I'm looking for a girl. She was in the fire."

"What is her name?"

"January MacLochlainn," I told her.

The girl typed on her keyboard and began shaking her head. "I'm sorry but there is no one here by that name."

"What?" I asked in disbelief. "Are you sure? Can you check again?" I asked, my body back to trembling status but this time in exponential form.

"Of course," she said and typed yet again. The expression on her face told me she'd gotten the same result.

"No, I'm sorry, sir. I have no one by that name. Can you describe her for me? There were several patients who couldn't be identified."

"Uh, she was wearing a black dress," I told the nurse. "She's about five ten, or, uh, two meters tall, long brown hair, green eyes." *She's amazing, unselfish, intelligent, sexy as hell. Her mere existence justifies mine.*

"Just a moment," she said and ran to the back.

Jason came up to me, his eyes asking me the news.

"They don't have anyone in their system with January's name," I explained, feeling like my body was on autopilot. "She's checking the patients who couldn't be identified."

Jason nodded.

I nervously paced the length of the receiving desk, running my fingers through the length of my hair over and over. Jason sat in a nearby chair, his thumbs drumming his thighs. Both our gazes were riveted by the doors for what felt like hours before the nurse came through with a smile on her face.

"She's here," she told us.

"Thank God," Jason told me, slapping his hands to his face.

The worry, anxiety and helplessness I'd felt for the past hour came flooding from my body and I collapsed to the floor, unable to hold myself up. She weakened me in every way possible.

"Christ," I whispered to the tile below me. My eyes filled with unshed tears and I fought to keep them in. I needed to see her.

Jason helped me as I struggled to my feet.

"How is she?" I asked when I had control of myself.

"She's in a room and resting comfortably. She was burned slightly on the hip and is awaiting a physician."

"Can I see her?

"Are you her spouse?"

"No, her- boyfriend."

"I'm sorry but you'll have to wait here until she's released then."

"Fine," I said, falling into a chair by the ER entrance.

Jason sat beside me.

"Jesus," Jason said simply beside me but the emotions of our ordeal were packed into the name.

"I know," I said, my body still trembling from the adrenaline.

We were silent for a few minutes, trying to recover from the worry.

"I thought I was going to lose..." I began to say but couldn't finish, choking on my words.

"Tom, it's cool now," Jason offered when I didn't continue.

I breathed deeply and let it out slowly. "I almost had her in there, Jason. I had her fingers in my hands but wasn't able to save her. I've failed her so miserably. I'm so ashamed of myself.

"If I had trusted her the way I should have from the beginning, I would have escorted her there instead of making her attend alone, making her search me out alone, making her save herself...alone."

"You can't beat yourself up, Tom. How would you have known the place was going to light up like the Fourth?"

"I can and I will. I let my past affect my future and I'd promised myself I wouldn't do that. I feel like a coward."

January

I was shivering cold in that hospital bed. The temperature coupled with the fact that I was burned and that my adrenaline was starting to wear off was making me shiver. When the nurse came in to tell me that Tom and Jason were out front and looking for me, I felt such extraordinary relief that they were okay that I started to cry, but that didn't mean I wanted to see Tom or even Jason for that matter.

Everything culminating in that moment before the fire was overwhelming and everything after was just plain cumbersome. Tears were the only relief I was being afforded in that moment because the hospital was busy I'd discovered after I'd woken and I was at the bottom of the priority totem pole. I'd have to wait for pain relief.

The burn wasn't that bad. I'd probably have a little bit of a scar there but not much else. My dress wasn't stuck to my body or anything. I'd been pushed against a railing near the source of the fire and couldn't pull myself away because the crowd was edging me against it. I was one of the first out and therefore sent to the hospital immediately after being checked for injuries.

About an hour after, I was aware that Tom was waiting for me, they moved my gurney out into the hall to treat some of the more pressing patients. It was another two hours before they saw and treated my minor burn. At four thirty in the morning, they discharged me right there in the hallway and not a moment too soon as I was getting ready to curse them out in French and walk out on my own.

I needed to decide what I was going to do about Tom. To be honest with you, I didn't even want to see his face. I wanted to walk right past him, flip him the bird for being so screwy with me and then head to my uncle's in Ireland. I knew I would quit that lousy job if I saw Jason within five feet of me but also knew that would be a bad idea. I needed the money. I needed the connections. One thing I could definitely not compromise though was working with Thomas Eriksson ever again.

Tom's treating me with such distance was one thing, something I could forgive. His leaving me to fend for myself at the club was something he would have needed a damn good excuse for and probably something I would have been able to listen to, but my near-death experience blew that chance right out the door.

My heart stopped in my chest. The decision had come without any consideration as to what it would do to my well-being. My brain wanted nothing to do with Tom any longer, but my heart screamed for me to run to him.

No, you've listened to your heart so much, January. It's time to be sensible. He's repeatedly shown you that he doesn't care for you the way you care for him. He's obviously still in love with Kelly. He's pulling away out of guilt.

I stood up and removed my hospital gown in the bathroom, replacing it with my sooty, torn couture masterpiece. *Oh well.* I walked with purpose out the double doors and into the lobby.

One foot in front of the other one, I deliberately avoided eye contact with the lobby and burst through the front doors of the ER. Just when my stomach was settling the worry Tom would find me, I heard his voice, making my heart jump into my throat.

"*January*?" he asked groggily. *Not a word from me, brother.*

I hailed a passing cab but he didn't stop. *Jerk.*

"January, are you okay?" he asked.

I sighed. Loudly. "I'm fine. Thanks for asking," I told him, an arm raised for an oncoming cab.

"Where are you going?" he asked, confused.

"As far away from you as I can get."

"Shit," he said under his breath. "January, please just hear me out. I-I'm an idiot."

I looked at him, a slight sarcastic smile on my face. "No, that's okay. I'm done with this toxic shit, Tom. I don't know what your problem is, frankly I don't care, but it's enough for me to realize that I better get out now, suffer the heartache and give myself a chance to find someone who won't ditch me or treat me like crap without talking to me about whatever's bothering him. I don't trust you anymore."

The cab pulled up beside me and I opened the door. Tom's hand came crushing over the edge, shutting it tight.

"Drive on!" He told the driver and the cab sped away.

"What the hell!" I yelled in his face, not in the mood for his games.

"Listen to me," he pleaded. "Just listen to me for a second."

"No way in hell." I used the classic women's "don't fuck with me" expression and he backed off a bit. I held up my hand for the next oncoming cab and it pulled up beside me. "You must mistake me for a sucker, Tom. I know exactly what's going on. You want out. You regret your time with me..."

"No!" He began but I cut him off with my hand.

"Listen, I get it. You're not over Kelly. You're feeling guilty about lying. You don't really love me and you don't want to lead me on. I've experienced this exact thing before. God, how I've experienced this same phenomenon over and over." I shook my head. "Whatever. I may not be the keepable type, but I will be okay without you, Tom."

And with those parting words, I left Tom slack-mouthed on the walk, closing the door behind me and giving the cabbie the name of the hotel. Tom began yelling at the cab and slamming his hands on the trunk, but I told the cabbie to step on it. I was going to be gone before he'd even know what happened and not a moment too soon either. I needed a place to hunker down for a while and hopefully ease the trouble I felt already brewing in my chest. I needed a reprieve from the impending doom and there was no better place than Donovan's.

The two-hour flight from Paris to Cork was excruciating. The more I tried to hold back the tears, the more they wanted to burn past my lids. My chest constricted with every breath I took. *So this is what real heartache is.* I finally understood why Tom became so bitter. There was nothing in the entire world like that feeling. Death would have been so much easier.

Donovan met me at the airport and I can honestly say I've never been so happy to see anyone in my life. The second I came within reach, I grabbed for him.

"Donny," I said quietly, the tears already streaming down my face.

"Ah, lass," he breathed out harshly. "Come," he said, hugging me tightly, "let's get to Killarney. You can tell me everythin' on the way."

The hourlong drive to Killarney provided barely enough time to let Donny in on the whole deal. He wasn't aware of the fire because I hadn't told anyone, not even my parents or siblings and he almost flipped out. What's the point in worrying them? I reassured him that it was just a minor burn and that over-the-counter meds would alleviate the pain, that's how minor it was.

Donny's street was a series of shops all connected into one seemingly long building with different facades peppering each shop. Donny lived above his own. The tears came down stronger at the sight of his little blue door.

"Oh now, stop it, love. It'll all be okay," Donny tried to soothe me.

I entered Donny's shop and sprinted up the stairs to his tiny apartment, bursting through the door and toppling onto his sofa.

"What the heavens!" I heard from the kitchen

I turned onto my back but kept the accent pillow at my face. In a sobbing voice, I said, "Hi, Aunt Briann."

"Is that my January?" she said, her singsong voice making me lose it more.

"Yes!" I wailed.

"Oh, my pet." She came to sit on the sofa arm and started rubbing my hair. "Donny told me a bit before he left. I'm sorry, love." She lifted me up by the shoulders. "Come on, January, let's get to your room. You can lie a bit and I'll wake you for dinner. I'll get

the rest from your uncle while you rest."
I nodded and she kissed my cheek because she couldn't reach my forehead. Aunt Briann was exceedingly beautiful and kind as hell. I don't know how surly Donny got her.

"Thank you, Briann."

Thomas

That cheeky wench had stunned me silent in front of that hospital. I'd been forced to gather my wits, but apparently I wasn't quick enough to catch her before she sped away. Jason informed me that night that January was on "vacation" in Killarney and that she'd return to New York City at the end of the week.

"The hell!" I told Jason as I packed my shit for a one-way flight to Cork.

"I thought Kelly's wedding was tomorrow," he said as I stuffed everything in my duffel.

"It is."

"You're going to miss it?"

"No, I'm going to swing by Killarney for Miss Assumption first and pick her up." Jason cleared his throat at my glaringly obvious contradiction. "Don't even start. I'm going to apologize for that," I told him. I'd informed Jason of everything that had gone on between January and me, including the phone call. "You're an idiot," he'd simply told me. "I know," I'd admitted. That was the end of that.

"Then I'll see you at the wedding?" he asked.

"Yes, with January in tow."

"Good," he'd said.

I rented a car in Cork and drove straight through to Killarney, reaching January's uncle's door at two in the morning. I parked quickly and at a weird angle, hoping to God no one attempted to drive down the narrow street, and started pounding on Donovan's door.

"January!" I yelled. "January! Open up!"

"Stop that poundin'!" A neighbor yelled from his window a few homes down.

"January!" I yelled, ignoring him. I repeatedly pounded again and again, desperate to see her.

The door whipped open just when I thought I couldn't take another second. "What are you *doing*?" A disheveled January asked me. God, she was glorious to look at!

She pulled me inside and closed the door. Her eyes were red and made me want to kick my own ass.

"January," I began, but she cut me off with a finger to her lips.

"Quiet, my aunt and uncle are asleep."

"Sorry." I reached for her but thought better of it and reigned my hands back in. "Please, January."

"Why are you here, Tom?" she asked, folding her arms across her attractive chest.

"I'm trying to explain to you what has been happening to me these past few days."

"I thought we already covered this," she spit out.

"No," I said, growing peeved. "Listen to me. Just let me explain, damn it!"

"Fine," she gritted.

I took a deep breath. "I'm in love with you, January."

"No, you're-"

"Stop! Just let me say this." She didn't say anything, so I continued. "I'm in love with you, but I need your forgiveness because I'm going to admit something I'm really ashamed of."

"Okay," she answered in hesitation.

She took a step back, wounding me, but I continued. "I, uh, I listened in on a conversation you had on the phone a few nights ago and I made some assumptions. I thought you were working with Jonah, letting him know our exact location. I thought you were two-timing me."

"I would never do that," she said simply.

"I know that," I confessed. "I should have come to you about it, but I was so angry and felt so betrayed, I-"

"Is that why you made me go to Reine alone?"

"Yes," I admitted.

Tears sprang to her eyes and I reached for her.

"No," she said, holding up her hands to stop me, breaking my heart. "Let me get this straight. You thought I was giving away our locations to that asshole and instead of coming to me and asking me about it, you assumed I was that untrustworthy, that my proclamation that I loved you was just bullshit?"

"It's shitty, I know, January."

"No," she said, laughing sarcastically. "What's shitty is that you thought I could fake all that. That every moment we'd ever shared on the road was not genuine." She shook her head. "That makes me sick to my stomach, Tom."

She ran her hands across her belly and stepped back. She wanted distance. I took hold of her, panicked she was about to say what I thought she was about to say.

"Don't," I said.

She brought her tear-filled eyes to mine. "But you already did. When you assumed I could be the type of person to do that, you admitted you didn't know me at all. How can you claim to love someone you don't know?"

"No," I told her, hugging her tighter, willing her to forgive me. "Don't, January. Please, I'm sorry. So, so sorry. Please," I begged, "I couldn't survive if *you* broke my heart."

"Stop," she said, openly bawling. "I've heard enough."

Crying, she began to push me toward the door, but I refused to move. I just couldn't accept that it was over. I refused to acknowledge it.

She stood tall and stepped back from me. "Get out," she whispered, continuing backward.

I watched as she inched her way to the stairwell and disappeared up the stairs. I was unmovable in the moment, my heart shattered at my feet and the one person capable of assembling the shards back into a working organ once more wanted nothing to do with me. And I deserved it.

I shuffled my leaden feet across the shop floor, closed the door behind me...

And pulled my hood over my head.

Chapter Twelve

This Too Shall Pass

New York City
Kelly's Wedding

Thomas

I walked into that wedding without a moment to spare. I say walked. I dragged my ass is more like it. Dragged because my body may as well have weighed as much as the Brooklyn Bridge for all the motivation I had to get out of bed.

Because January left me. She fucking left me and it was all my fault. For the first time in my entire life, I knew what it truly meant to be in love with someone, to know exactly who you're meant to be with, and never having a chance in hell of reconciling what you never intended to fuck up.

I found my family and squeezed in next to Harper while the organ played.

"Oh, Jesus! You scared me!" Harper said, grasping her chest. She hugged me fiercely and kissed my cheek. A small tear escaped her eye. "It's so good to see you, friend."

"You have no idea," I said, hugging her back.

I stood and hugged all my friends, lingering a bit at Cherry.

"My lovely Cherry, how are you?"

"I have never been happier to see you in all my life," she admitted, "but you look like shit." She peered around me. "Where's your girl, baby?" The expression on my face must have revealed it all and her smile fell. I shook my head. "Oh, Tommy. It'll be okay. Let me help you fix this."

"It can't be fixed," I whispered as Callum slapped my shoulder in greeting.

"My God, Tom. I've found it very difficult to handle these women without you. We've taken a vote. You can't leave again."

This made me smile but it was unpracticed and he could tell something was wrong.

"You've been dumped," he said.

Harper approached our little pow-wow and grabbed her husband's hand, making my chest constrict at the idea that January and I could have been just like them. Perfect.

"*You have*?" Harper yells, before bringing her voice back down. "What the devil, Tom? Seriously?"

"Yeah, I have."

Cherry wound her arm through mine and brought me close to her side. "We're going to fix it, Tom."

She said it so confidently, I almost believed her.

"Yes," Harper agreed just as strongly. "It must be a mistake. Thomas Eriksson doesn't get dumped. Girls should clamor in line to be with you."

I smiled at her but couldn't answer. Truth be told, I'd buried myself the second I didn't trust January the way she deserved to be. I let my old cynical self take over and although I promised her I'd be good to her, I'd failed her.

Callum looked on his wife and kissed her temple. You could tell he was proud of her, of her loyalty. She was amazing. All the girls were. I'd need them to help me survive.

"Enough about me, lovelies. This is Kelly's day. Let's not detract from her." I was obviously deflecting and they knew it but decided to let it go...for then.

The ceremony was beautiful as was the bride. I reveled in the fact that six months prior I wouldn't have even considered showing up the day of the wedding, let alone being lovesick, for real, for an entirely different girl. I laughed to myself as I gazed on Kelly walking down the aisle and felt nothing more than admiration for a very good friend. Then I thought of January and imagined it was *her* timing her steps on the arm of *her* father. That idea sent a new wave of hurt to emanate through my chest and heart.

That was the moment I knew January should have been *my* very own bride. The thought of her marching toward another made me queasy and I had to grip the pew in front of me for support.

The next night, we all sat around Cherry's deck. (Charlie's apartment was now known as Cherry's. That's always how those things go, I think.) We were all drinking, except for Carter and Kelly of course, as they'd left for Fiji that morning. I couldn't help but feel a small sense of peace around my extended family. Harper sat on Callum's lap as they laughed as some private joke. Charlie slowly danced with Cherry. Marty, Aaron, Nat, Jared and Josiah all sat around singing, passing a bottle of wine around. Freddy, Sam, Cross and SO were inside playing a serious game of Scrabble.

I wasn't happy, but I was as close as I was going to get to feeling a semblance of normality. *Yeah, in order for you to avoid going over the deep end, dude, you're going to have to move in with your married friends. You're fucking pathetic.*

A buzzing, ringing sound interrupted my thoughts. *My phone*. I barely recognized the ringtone; I hadn't used it in so long. I dug it out of my pocket and pulled down my hoodie to answer, not bothering to check who it was.

"Hello?" I asked.

"Yo, it's Jason."

"Hey, J. What are you up to?"

He sighed. Not a good sign. "Nothing, man. I just needed to talk to you. Are you at Cherry's?"

"*Shit.* Just say whatever it is you have to say." My gut clenched in preparation.

"I'd really feel better if-"

"Jason, don't effing make me wait. Just spit it out."

"They gave Jonah the position."

Of course they did.

"I see."

"There were a lot of deciding factors-"

"Cut the bullshit, Jason. You and I are friends, good friends at that. No need to give me the whole song and dance after ten years. Now come over and pick me up. We're going out. And bring a bottle of Jack for later."

When you can't have what you want, drinking always helps...kind of. Not really. But who the hell cares.

I kissed the girls goodbye when Jason rang me from downstairs. "Bye, Cherry Bomb," I said to her at the door, but she pulled me in for a last minute pep talk.

"Don't do anything stupid, Tommy Boy. You'll regret it and you'll spin down a shame spiral the likes of which we've never seen. I know you, and right now, you're hellbent on causing irreparable damage. Just stop and think, baby."

"I'll try, Cher," I said, kissing her forehead but even I knew that was a lie.

I took the stairs to the lobby and hopped in the cab with Jason. "Let's get shitfaced."

"Just what the doctor ordered," Jason said, pulling out a bottle of Jack from the floorboard. "Let's drop this off at my pad and then hit the city."

After dropping the liquor off at Jason's, we headed to Soho.

"Let's make some bad decisions," Jason said, clapping his hands together as we took two stools at the bar.

"Yeah," I said, feeling uncomfortable already. I needed to drown that feeling out pronto.

"What'll it be?" the bartender asked.

"Scotch, McEwan's," Jason said, ordering for me.

"No!" I protested, an image of January in Dublin coming to the front of my mind. "No." I cleared my throat. "Uh, two shots of Patron, please."

The bartender nodded.

Six shots later and I was starting to lose sensation in my gums. This was a good thing. I needed to forget, needed the torn and gaping hole in my effing chest to feel numb. Jason was dancing with a girl on the other side of the bar and all I could think was that I needed to keep drinking.

"Is this seat taken?" a gorgeous blonde asked me.

"Go 'head," I slurred.

"What are you drinking?" she asked.

"Patron," I told her.

My forearms had permanent dents in them from resting so harshly against the wooden bar top. She leaned into me slightly and I pushed them in further.

"Is that your friend over there?"

"Yeah."

"He's dancing with my friend."

"Cool."

"Why aren't you dancing?" she asked, leading.

"I'm not the dancing type." That wasn't true. For January, I was.

"Can I get a Patron for my friend here?" she asked the bartender.

She stood so I could get full view of her figure. She was beautiful, very, yet she was nothing.

"I can buy my own drinks," I told her.

"You've obviously been through something." She sidled even closer and I was too drunk to keep her off. "It's written all over your face," she whispered closely. Her sickly sweet perfume enveloped me. "Let me help you forget," she suggested, running her hand up my forearm. The touch made me sick to my stomach.

There was a time in my life where a woman like this would have been warm in my bed within the hour of meeting her. There was a time I would do those sordid things and feel almost nothing at all for it. I looked at her closely in that second and she mistook it for interest, smiling at me kindly. All I could see and think when I looked on her was that this young woman was someone's daughter, sister, possibly mother. I was disgusted with myself knowing all this time I'd been acting like the biggest fool at the expense of so many girls. I realized I'd caused untold damage. I didn't deserve January.

Yet looking at that girl, knowing what she was willing

to do with me, I knew I would never do those things again, and not because I cared one iota for that girl. No, it was because I could never betray January like that. I loved January more than I loved myself and that was the first time I'd ever really felt that way for someone. I knew it would probably be the only time.

I was going to stay away from January MacLochlainn...because I loved her more than anyone on God's green earth and she deserved someone as amazing as herself.

"What's your name?" I asked the blonde.

"Kristi," she smiled.

"Kristi, would you have sex with me tonight?" I asked honestly.

Her smile faltered for a moment but picked right back up. "Yes, I would," she said quietly.

"Why?"

"I-I don't know."

"I know why," I told her, "because you don't know your own worth. Some advice?" I stood up and gathered my hoodie, throwing it over my shoulders. "Discover *why* you're important, then refuse to settle for anyone who doesn't completely agree."

I walked out of the busy bar, sucking in cool New York air and wishing to everything that I was going home to January because January *was* my home. I texted Jason, letting him know I bailed and I'd see him around, that I was heading to L.A. the next day.

I was running away, for real this time.

Six weeks later...
Thomas

L.A. was a fucking mess. I found a dozen bands worth signing and sent them Jason's way, but I was so miserable, I barely remembered any of them. I was mechanical, even more than Austin Tom. Austin Tom was downright cheery compared to Los Angeles Tom.

In Austin, I was pissed off. Los Angeles, I was practically suicidal, depressed as hell and nearly crying into my damn pillow every single night like a damn girl. I was miserable. Every corner I turned, I thought I saw January. Every time I bought a coffee, went jogging, grocery shopping, I could smell her, hear her, feel her. She seemed to be everywhere I wanted her to be but not tangible enough to touch or kiss her. She was seared into my brain.

A month and a half into my stay, I knew I needed to see her. I just needed to drink her in, to soothe the ragged edges of my soul and just memorize her one more time. I'd do it every month if I had to. Eventually weaning myself free in a few weeks, months, okay, years.

I needed a plan.

And that plan came in the form of a phone call from Jason.

"Dude, we need you in New York," he told me over a broken line.

"What? Why?"

"Let's just say, the shiteth hath hitteth the fan."

"Shut the eff up. What's going on?"

"Just get your ass here. I'll tell you all about it on Monday."

I wasn't going to fight it. A free ticket to New York? And I'd self-diagnosed myself dehydrated of January MacLochlainn. Time for your meds, Tom.

Take two Januarys a day and call me in the morning.

New York

"Thank God!" Jason said to me as I exited my cab. I'd called a few minutes before and told him I was coming. He'd told me he'd meet me street level. This meant news to Jason. I found him smoking a cigarette. He put it out with his shoe by the time I'd closed the cab door.

"Are you going to tell me what's going on now?"

"No," he said succinctly. "Come with me."

"Jeez, I'm pretty effing tired of these cryptic messages from you. Last time this happened, I got stuck doing something I didn't want to do."

"Oh, come now. Last time I checked, you found your soul mate in that little incident. Don't knock unanswered prayers, brotha!"

"Yeah, look how happy I am now."

"Just shut up. I'm about to make your fucking day."

We rode the rest of the elevator ride in silence. The doors opened to the executive floor and I felt an incredible sense of deja' vu as we made our way to Peter Weathervane's office. Jason knocked.

"Come in!" I heard Peter yell.

I don't know what I expected when I entered Peter's office. Maybe Jonah drumming his fingers like the evil freak he was? It sure as hell wasn't Peter's latest wife sitting on his lap.

"Shit! Sorry," I began. *Wait, he invited you in.*

"No worries. She was just leaving."

His wife pretended to pout and he handed over a credit card, making me want to gag. *January would* never *do that kind of shit*. She strutted out of his office, her short skirt barely covering her ass. She smiled at me seductively as she left. *Well, that was disgusting*.

"Tom!" Peter said, finishing off his drink and standing. He tucked in his disheveled shirt and I almost lost my lunch. No telling what they were doing before we walked in. "I, uh, I'm not good at apologies." He looked thoughtful a moment. "Matter of fact, I don't think I've ever apologized to anyone before. Huh. Anyway, listen, Jonah's gone. You're the new R&D rep. Congrats."

He sat down and picked up the phone. He was done with us.

Jason ushered us out of the room and closed the door behind us.

"What the hell just happened there?" I asked Jason.

"Congrats, Tom."

"Thanks? I'm confused."

"Jonah's gone. Turns out you were the right man for the job all along. I'd told Peter that a million times but he's such a stickler for his own stupid rules...Anyway, congrats."

"I'm wiggin' out here, Jason."

"Stop questioning it. Just roll with it, dude."

I thought about it for a moment. "Fine. I mean, this is fantastic news. Everyone will love that I'm here to stay."

"Speaking of everyone," he said. "Come with me."

We took the elevator down two floors down and I absently remarked that Peter never did apologize, though for what, I didn't know. Jason thought that hilarious.

"Follow me," Jason coolly said, walking past the floor receptionist and waving.

I gazed at all the office doors on that floor and noted they were all a serious frosted glass and ten feet high. "What exactly is my new salary?" I asked Jason, staring at the names on the plates beside each door.

We stopped at the last one on the floor and it read *Thomas Eriksson*. I almost burst out laughing.

"I had Suzanne rush that for you."

"Who the hell is Suzanne?"

"Your secretary. It's six figures."

"Huh?" I asked, inspecting my nameplate.

"Your salary? It's six figures."

"Shut the eff up," I told him as he swung the door to my office open.

"Surprise!" I heard in chorus.

Inside my barren office was my entire family. My mom, dad, sister, Cherry and Charlie, Callum and Harper, and all the rest of the gang, including Kelly and Carter. My eyes began to sting with how happy I was to see them all in one place and I shook it away, clearing my throat. Harper was closest and threw her arms over my neck.

"Tom, congratulations!" She told me, tears streaming down her face.

"Thank you," I choked back. "Thank you, everyone."

I noticed my mom in the corner and pushed my way to her. "Mom," I said, hugging her tightly.

I felt like a little kid. I needed my mom so badly in that moment. I needed her to tell me it was all going to be okay.

"Congratulations, my darling boy," she said, and I could feel her tears fall on my shoulder.

"I love you, Mom."

"I love you too."

"Dad," I said, moving to him and hugging him fiercely. "It's so good to see you."

"Congrats, son."

I looked around and swallowed the faces surrounding me. The love and admiration from each of them was so incredibly humbling. Everyone I loved was in that room. Every single one save for the one I loved the most.

Knock. Knock.

We all froze where we stood, unsure what to do.

"Answer it, you dolt!" Cherry playfully jeered, making everyone laugh.

I opened the door and was stunned silent.

"Uh, hi," January MacLochlainn told me.

She was just as stunning as I'd memorized her to be, if not more so. She'd trimmed her hair since last I saw her and her skin was a bit less tan. She wasn't any better put together or anything but she obviously wasn't being forced to improvise on the road. She had access to a permanent wardrobe.

She was unbelievably beautiful. I'd wondered what she'd been doing since I last saw her. I wanted to throw her into my arms and kiss her senseless but I didn't. I couldn't. She wasn't mine to throw.

"Hi," I stupidly replied after too long a silence. Things were awkward.

"I-I just wanted to stop by and congratulate you. Everyone's really excited to have you back," she said, then cleared her throat. "Anyway, I see you're busy," she said, popping her head in the room and smiling at everyone. "I won't bother you anymore. It was nice to see you again." She waved to everyone in the room then left.

I closed the door behind her, dumbstruck. No, struck mute, like a complete idiot. She'd left me tongue-tied. I knew if I had opened my mouth I would have just spouted nonsense or worse, proclaim that I loved her again but at the top of my lungs and in front of my entire family.

I turned toward that family and caught a sea of shocked faces with mouths agape.

I swallowed as I took them all in. "What?" I asked, breaking the silence.

"Was that her?" Cherry asked quietly.

"Yeah, that was January."

All the girls yelped at once, startling me.

"What!" I yelled.

"Go after her!" Harper commanded. "Right now!"

"*What*?"

"Are you *nuts*? *That's* the January you couldn't shut up about?" My dad interjected, the complete surprise etched all over his aging face.

"Yeah," I sang, more nervous than I'd ever been.

Callum slapped me on the shoulder. "If you don't go after that girl, Tom, I believe these women may skin you alive."

"What do I do?" I asked them, desperation seeping into my voice.

"Do you know how you got this job?" Jason asked evenly, interrupting the already conspiring females. He stared absently out the window before turning toward me.

Everyone grew quiet.

"No," I said truthfully.

"Can you not guess?"

"I have no clue." I was being honest. I had no idea. I figured Jonah had quit or thrown himself off a bridge. I didn't care. *What*?

"January."

"January got me the job?" I asked, baffled as ever.

"Yes, January put her own reputation on the line to save your sorry ass."

"How?" I swallowed audibly.

"She went to Peter Weathervane, without permission, by the way." We both knew that showing up unannounced at Peter's door is basically a death wish. I nodded. "Turns out, January found she was somewhat responsible for Jonah thieving all your bands."

"She'd never do that," I said, defending her.

"No, not directly," Jason continued, fishing his cigarette and lighter out of his pocket, as if he could smoke it in there. He was nervous just talking about the risk January took. I breathed deeply. "Apparently, when she would phone home, she'd let them know where she was going and I guess Jonah found this out somehow. He'd ring her home soon after claiming to represent the label and conned her little sister into spilling your locations.

"She felt awful about it, I guess, and risked her own job to let Peter know the truth. When Peter confronted Jonah with the phone records, he couldn't deny it and was fired on the spot."

"Oh my God, she could have been fired as well."

"I know," Jason said.

"Why?" my mom asked.

"Because our locations were label business and we signed confidentiality agreements before we'd left. We don't want competition from other labels. She risked herself for me."

"What a brave girl," Kelly said. "She must love you very much."

I was staggered by Kelly's words and could only stand there, staring at my shoes.

"I have to find her," I said suddenly and bolted out the door.

Everyone followed me out into the hall.

"Wait!" I heard Jason say from behind me. "Don't you want to know where to find her?"

I turned back around.

"She's a producer now."

"No kidding," I said, happy to hear it, walking backward for a bit before turning back around.

"What does that mean?" I heard my mom ask my dad as I ran for the elevator doors.

"It means she's a talented, talented girl," I heard my pop explain to my mom, making me smile. I'd used those exact same words to describe her to Jason in Austin just in a very different context. I had no idea at the time just how true those words really were.

I hit the buttons for the below ground floor on the elevator and my body shook in anticipation.

Cherry came skidding to a halt next to me as the doors slid open and I stepped inside, turning to face her.

"Be patient, Tommy," She told me. "Remember to be patient."

I nodded as the doors slipped closed.

The ride down was excruciating. My heart could keep time with a hummingbird's wing and the sweat began to slide down my neck. I'd never been so nervous in all my life.

Ding.

I startled. *Get it together*. I practically sprinted down the hall towards the studios and was brought short by none other than Georgia Asher.

"Georgia!"

"Good God, man!" she said before realizing it was me. "Oh! Thomas!" she said properly, making me smirk. "What are you doing here?"

"I'm looking for January. Have you seen her?"

Georgia's shoulders sank in my hands. "I'm afraid she's left for the night. She came into the studio a few minutes ago complaining she wasn't feeling well. She's taken off."

"Right," I said, kissing Georgia's cheek. "See you around."

"Bye then!" she said, waving at me with a sweet smile. I loved Georgia.

I returned to my office deflated. When I opened my door, I was bombarded by women.

"What happened? Where is she? What's going on?" They all chimed in at once.

"Give the guy some room!" Callum said.

I backed off a bit and rubbed my forehead, leaning against the edge of my new desk. "She wasn't there. She left for the day, said she felt ill."

"She's not ill," Cherry said.

All the girls seemed to agree, including my mom.

"She's upset," Harper added, nodding happily. "This is good."

"*What*? That's awful!" I told them.

"No, it's a good sign," my mom said. "It means she's not over you. This is a very good sign."

I gulped. "What should I do?" I asked them.

"We go to her."

"I don't know where she lives."

"How is that possible?" Jason asked.

"It never came up!" I seethed.

"Fine, I could get into trouble for this, but I'll look it up. Be right back."

Jason left to do his thing and everyone visibly relaxed.

"What should I say to her?"

"Tell her you love her," Kelly suggested.

"What if she doesn't want me?"

"Patience, Tom," Cherry said again. "She does love

you. Pride's getting in the way, for both of you, it seems."

"Tell her you know she still loves you," my sister Christina said. "Tell her you know what she did for you. That it's your proof."

"Okay," I said, absorbing it all.

I backed up some more when the women started studying me more closely. "What? You're making me nervous."

"Unzip your jacket," Marty said, "and remove the hood."

I did as she said.

"Better," Cherry said, examining me.

"Don't. That's it. I'm done. She'll listen to me regardless of the way I'm dressed."

"That's a very good thing," my mom said, making all the girls laugh.

"I-I, uh, need a moment," I said, feeling stifled.

I burst into the hall and breathed in the air, running my hands through my hair. I was beginning to suffocate with all the estrogen flowing in that room.

"Just be yourself," I heard from behind me. Callum.

I was so grateful he'd joined me. "You think?"

"Yeah, just tell her how you truly feel, leave nothing out, trust me about that, and leave the rest up to fate," he said, leaning his body against the hall wall.

"Thanks," I told him, running my hands through my hair.

"Anytime."

"I've got it!" Jason yelled down the hall.

Just as suddenly, my office door clicked open and a sea of people came barreling my way. I barely had enough time to react as they ushered me in front of them, pushing me toward the elevator.

"You're not all coming with me!" I yelled.

"Oh yes we are!" Cherry shouted from the back of the crowd.

"You're not serious!" I said, stopping in front of them and taking in the sheer number. We wouldn't even fit in one elevator car.

"We are!" someone shouted.

"Fine, but you're all waiting down the street."

I led the group of fifteen to the trains and we all piled in.

"This is ridiculous," I said under my breath.

"Yes, it is," Cherry agreed, "but if life wasn't ridiculous sometimes, what kind of life would it be?"

"A normal one," I countered playfully.

"Hush it," she said, prodding my shoulder with hers. "You love it."

I did.

"It's gonna be a long train ride home if she says no," Jason said after a few minutes.

"Shut up, Jason!" the girls said in unison.

"Jeez Louise!" he said, smiling deviously.

"Oh my God, she's gonna say no," I said, beginning to hyperventilate.

Harper sent Jason a death glare. "No, she won't."

"How do you know?"

"Because I just do, Tom."

Apparently January's grandma's house was only a ten-minute walk from the station so we decided to hoof it. Every step I took January's direction made my body shake impossibly worse than the last.

January's home was a typical Jersey split level, baby blue and ugly as hell. I stood just down the street from it, my family flanking me and immediately feeling for all the world like an absolute idiot for agreeing to bring them along.

"You all wait right here," I said with conviction, eyeing them all harshly. "I swear to God, if I see one of you girls anywhere near us, I'll have your prospective spouses whip you, fifties-style."

"Ugh!" Marty yelped. I focused in on her and she pretended to zip her mouth.

"Stay. Here."

I nervously walked January's way and shook out my hands to steady them, wiping the sweat onto the thigh of my jeans. I scaled the sidewalk to the front door. My finger lingered over the doorbell.

"Here goes nothing."

Chapter Thirteen

Settle Down

January

I'd barely rinsed the conditioner from my hair when I heard the doorbell. I'd hopped in the shower almost immediately after coming home. I needed two things. One, I needed privacy so I could bawl my eyes out after seeing Tom at Seven where he proceeded to blow me off, making me feel worse than I ever thought I could. Two, I needed the water to soothe myself and my aching heart.

Who could that be? I thought as the doorbell rang again. I shrugged my shoulders and continued to cry into the falling water, sniffling like a little girl. They could sit on the porch for all I cared.

"You!" I heard loudly.

I turned the water off and stilled, listening for the commotion coming from the direction of the living room.

"You don't understand!" I heard my cousin Collin say loudly.

I hopped out of the shower quickly and wrapped my short robe around myself. Hauling ass outside of the bathroom, almost slipping on the wood in the hallway. Sounds of fighting came from the front lawn along with...*chanting*? I ran to the front door and stepped out onto the front porch.

"What's going on?" I asked, stopping still at the sight of Tom's hands around Collin's neck. "Tom?" I could feel the burn of tears beginning to surface again. "What-what's going on?"

"January," he said desperately, releasing his grip on my cousin and coming toward me. He stood on the bottom step beneath me.

Collin fell to the grass, rubbing his neck. "Do you know him?" he asked.

"Yeah, this is Tom," I explained, gesturing towards Tom like an idiot. Collin started laughing.

"What?" we both asked, turning his direction.

"This guy thought I was your boyfriend. He said he recognized me from the airport and told me I couldn't have you, that you belonged to him."

"Tom," I sighed, realizing for the first time I was standing on my porch in a short ass robe, naked underneath and hair dripping in front of fifteen random people. "Can I talk to you inside?" I asked.

"Yeah," he said, climbing the porch steps.

I glanced behind me and saw a guy who looked exactly like Tom but older.

"Who are those people?" I asked quietly, as we entered my grandmother's home.

"Uh, those are my parents and sister and friends."

"Great, I just embarrassed myself in front of your entire family."

"I'm so sorry, January," he said, running his hands over his face and through his hair. "This was not how this was supposed to go."

I led him into my room and shut the door. "You attacked my cousin."

"About that," Tom said, sighing deeply. "I'm so sorry," he began but stopped short when I burst out laughing. "What?"

"Nothing, I just- never mind. Why are you here?"

Tom stood tall and stepped closer to me, grabbing my shoulders in the process. "I'm in love with you, January MacLochlainn, and I want you to take me back."

The tears had already started flowing. I couldn't stop them. His mere touch was enough to break me down. "Why?"

"Because you love me as well."

"No, I don't," I lied.

"Yes, you do."

My head fell toward my feet and a soft sob escaped my lips. "You hurt me so badly, Tom. For weeks, I felt like I had to tiptoe around you. I was walking on eggshells and when I finally felt comfortable enough to stomp around, you pulled the rug out from under me. I don't think I could take another surprise like that. It's not healthy, no matter how much I'm in love with you."

"January," he said, hugging me closely. Irrationally, I worried that my hair would soak his shirt. "I am so sorry for not trusting you in Europe. I never really believed you would betray me like that. I think I was just scared of what you are to me."

"And what am I to you?" I asked, looking up into his blue eyes.

"You're the love of my life, January MacLochlainn," he said without shame.

He ran his hands along my forehead and down my face, stopping at my collarbone. He stared at me like I was the last woman on Earth.

And the tears came in droves. "Don't say things like that to me, Tom."

"I'm not just saying them because I think that's what you want to hear. I'm telling you this because it's the truth. I can't live without you, J. You're it. You're *it*. Get me?"

I nodded, afraid to speak. He took me in his arms and brought me closer, inching me nearer to his chest slowly as if he was frightened I'd spook. His eyes searched my face like he was drinking me in for the last time. "God, I love you," he said without thinking.

He brought his mouth to mine and I could feel the desperation he felt for me. It matched mine completely. I grazed my hands up his shoulders and wrapped them around his neck. Staring at him afforded me the first sense of peace I'd felt in the weeks since I last saw him.

His lips moved over mine languidly and I felt drunk from the warmth of his breath. His bottom lip trembled against mine in restraint and I decided to give him the permission he was begging for.

I pressed the kiss deeper, breathing in deeply through my nose. I was on the brink of ecstasy. *Incredible*, I thought. I broke free a moment and told him how I felt before diving back in.

"January," he whispered, sending a thrill up my arms and legs, where it pooled in my belly.

His tongue stung sweetly and I realized I wanted to be the only one who would be able to taste him *forever*. We edged slowly toward the bed, never breaking the kiss and toppled onto my disheveled quilt. Tom was wedged between my legs and my robe came undone a little, the edge of my breasts exposed.

We stopped for just a moment, realizing where things were headed. His eyes roamed my entire body before he ran the backs of two fingers over the exposed skin at my chest. "You're so beautiful, January," he told me.

I brought him closer to me and I kissed him fiercely. I was ready for him.

"I want you," I told him.

"I want you too," he said, kissing me deeper.

His right hand followed the line of my body starting at my shoulders, his thumb cupping underneath my breast before continuing down, pinching my hip and holding the back of my thigh, bringing my leg up and around him.

This seemed to bring something out in me but stilled him. I peppered his face and neck with kisses.

"What's wrong?" I asked him.

"This isn't right," he told me, but his body told me differently.

"It doesn't feel wrong," I told him, sucking on the lobe of his ear.

"January," he moaned before sitting up and bringing me with him.

I continued to kiss him and he kissed me back. He wanted this but he was fighting me the entire way.

"January," he said softly, kissing the side of my neck. "This secret I've yet to earn. It's not right for me to learn you yet. Please," he said, kissing my forehead, "I can't do to you what I've done with the others. I owe you so much more than that. You're worth so much more."

A heated embarrassment painted my entire body. "I'm so sorry," I said, wrapping the robe tighter around my torso, feeling so ashamed of myself.

Tom stood and adjusted his clothing before helping me to my feet. He brought me close to him and hugged me, kissing the top of my head. "Don't be sorry," he said, running his hands down my back. "There's nothing to be sorry about. We're just going to do this right, is all." He eyed me with a slight smirk. "It'll be hard as hell, but I'm determined."

"Thank you," I told him sincerely.

"No, thank you," he said, kissing my temple.

I startled when someone knocked on my door.

"January?" I heard Grandma Betty say on the other side.

Tom panicked but I stifled laughter.

"Yes, Maimeó?"

"Are you in there alone with a boy?" she asked.

"Yes, Maimeó, but we're behaving," I told her truthfully, running my hand along the side of Tom's face, he buried it in my hand and kissed my palm.

"All the same, young lady...out."

This time we both laughed. "Yes, Maimeó."

"Also, there's 'bout fifteen people sittin' out on our front lawn. Would you know anythin' about that?"

Chapter Fourteen
The Gambler

Six months later...
Thomas

"Move your hand a little to the left," the photographer told me.

January and I were at a photo shoot for *Junkie,* a national music mag doing a piece on the people who helped shape the bands America knows and loves. We were honored, to say the least, because we were being featured in the article and might even earn the cover. Apparently, they were impressed.

They'd done a short interview a few weeks prior already and it was time for the shoot. They'd done a few posed shots and told us to take a minute while they made some adjustments to the set.

I threaded my hands through January's while we waited.

"What do you want to do tonight?" I asked her. She playfully leaned back, forcing me to hold her body weight upright for her. I couldn't help but laugh at her.

"I'm not sure. What do you want to do?" she asked, bringing her face up, her nose near mine and wiggling her brows.

I swung her in my arms and she laughed out loud.

"You mean besides you?"

"Stop," she laughed.

"How about we grab a bottle and meet the gang for a game or something."

"Yeah, that's it. That's what we're doing tonight." January got on with my friends better than I did, it seemed. "Well, that and making out."

I grinned at her. "Oh, you'd like to make out with me, J?" I asked, wrapping my arms around her waist and blowing into her neck.

She laughed. "Hell yeah I do."

Music was playing in the room so I swung her in my arms and began dancing with her, shifting her from side to side. Her hair swayed across the hand I had splayed against her back and I felt her shiver at my touch. God, how she affected me with her reactions.

"How about we skip the wine, our friends and the game and go right to the make out part."

"Okay," she said in a silly voice.

I attacked her neck with my lips, following up her jaw and kissing her lips softly and slowly. Lazily, taking my sweet ass time, I tasted her tongue, running my own against the ridge of her teeth.

"I love you, January," I said, when the kiss broke.

"I love you too, Tom."

I ran my hands down her face and lightly squeezed

her cheeks, puckering her lips a little. I kissed them and brought my hands down.

That's when we realized we had an audience, and a large one at that. January's face lit up to impossible shades of red and I instinctively tucked her into my side.

"Sorry, we didn't realize you were waiting," I apologized.

"It's okay," the photographer smiled, as he put up his camera "you're done. You're free to go."

"Oh," January said, "but I thought - never mind. Cool."

We wrapped up the shoot and decided to head to my apartment. Grandma Betty's wasn't exactly conducive to make out sessions, if that wasn't already obvious. My lease was up a few weeks after I got the R&D position and January helped me move into my own place. Yeah, it was a studio, but it was mine and I'd never had anything to myself before.

"When do the mags come out?" January asked, rummaging through my fridge for a Coke.

"Next month, on the first. They're sending us our own box."

What I hadn't told January and for a very good reason was that I ensured they'd go to her studio on a day I knew we'd both be there because this magazine wasn't just an article on what we did for Seven. Oh no, it was much, much more.

"Oh, cool," she said, popping the top off the glass bottle in her hand.

"Come here," I said, tossing myself on my bed and flipping the stereo on.

She took a swig and set the bottle on the bar before coming over and cuddling into my side.

"I like this," she said getting comfortable and kissing my neck.

Get used to it, I thought.

We kissed for hours. I didn't know how many more make out sessions I was going to be able to endure. I found her fascinating and every time I touched her, I felt more and more drawn to her.

"Come on," I told her later as she was falling asleep.

She groaned in displeasure. "Let me just sleep here," she complained.

"No, come on. I'll take you to Sam's." Sam's is where January would sleep sometimes on the weekends. Sam didn't care because she was barely there and I had peace of mind at Sunday night dinners with Grandma Betty and her curious eyes. That woman saw all. Especially since our last "conversation."

"Fine," she huffed, blowing her hair out of her eyes and sitting up.

I looked on her. "Just a few more minutes," I conceded, making her smile.

She fell into my arms and all felt right with the world.

April 1st, the next month
Thomas

I took extra special care to look nice that day. I wore the suit I wore to Callum and Harper's wedding and even went to the trouble of buying new black Converse for the occasion. I cut my hair, but not so much that I couldn't still tuck it behind my ears.

That entire morning I paced back and forth in my office. Suzanne asked if I wanted decaf and I told her that I wanted nothing. She kept looking at me with this worried expression. It made me want to laugh. My office felt stifling, so I cracked the window at the top of my ceiling with one of those circulating bars. I played with that thing so much when I first got there, I thought it was going to break. It was probably the only thing that kept me from messing with it so much.

I turned on a few tunes, thought better of it and shut them off then rethought that as well and picked a few Max Richter songs to rotate at a low volume instead. I messed with the pillows on my sleek black leather sofa a million times before finally realizing January wouldn't even notice. I had Suzanne dust my long windowsill and water the plants the day before and those looked good.

I was just straightening my Warhol print when I heard January's lively voice telling everyone around her hello. My entire body went bloody warm and my hands began to shake. I sat in my chair and picked up a book, thought twice and pretended to be working on my computer.

"Hello, Suzanne!" I heard her say and I had to clench my jaw shut to keep it from chattering.

"Hi, Miss MacLochlainn. You can go right in!"

"Thank you!" January said before bursting into my office like a breath of fresh air.

"Howdy!" she said, dancing into my office, swinging a cardboard box around.

"Hi, babe," I spit out, barely.

"*They're here*!" she sang, plopping the box onto my desk.

She took the scissors from the cup on my desk and opened them so the sharp part was exposed. She ran the length through the tape binding the entire thing and I swear to God I thought I could hear my heartbeat in my ears. I stood quickly and shut the door before sitting back down in my chair. I tried to rest my hand on my mouse but it was trembling so badly, I pretended I needed something from my shelf. I stood, retrieved the tape, *the tape?*, then sat back down. Thankfully, she didn't notice and I abandoned the worthless tape in front of me.

I set my arms on the rests of the chair and folded my quaking hands over my stomach.

"Ooh!" she exclaimed, making me sit up a bit. "We're on the cover after all!" She drank in the image of us and turned it toward me. "Oh my God," she breathed.

I somehow brought my face down from staring at her eyes and noticed the pic they'd chosen. It was January and me, but not in one of the posed shots like I expected. In fact, it was a candid shot of us when we thought no one was watching. We were both laughing, my face almost buried in her neck, and her hair falling back. We looked so incredibly happy.

I swallowed.

"Can you believe how beautiful this shot is, Tom?" she asked.

"Yes," I said matter-of-factly. "You're in it."

"Tom," she choked, a small tear escaping her eye. She smiled gently, wiped it clear of her face and took a steadying breath. She flipped open the magazine and took a seat in the chair at the foot of my desk. She brought her feet up and crossed her ankles on the glass.

"Let's see," she said, looking up the index.

Oh my word, here we go, I thought.

She looked at me like she'd only just noticed me and smiled again, making my heart stutter. "Well, don't you look smart today," she said before standing up and kissing me, then sitting back down.

I think I'm going to have a heart attack. "Th-thank you," I stuttered but she was too distracted to notice.

"Okay," she said, "page seventy-nine. Seventy-nine," she repeated, flipping through the pages. My knee bounced rapidly and my hand slapped down to still it.

She looked up at the noise. "You okay, buttercup?"

"Uh-huh," I offered.

"*Okay,*" she sang and went back to searching. "Sixty-eight," she teased. "Seventy-two." My heart beat rapidly in my chest. "Ah! Here we are. Seventy-nine."

She turned the page and saw that we had a two-page spread. Minutes seemed to pass.

Her face fell and tears started to fall when she read the header. She brought quivering hands to her face and looked at me with glassy eyes.

I stood and fished the wooden box from my right pocket.

"January MacLochlainn," I said, kneeling on my left knee in front of her, "I love you so incredibly much." A sob burst from her mouth but she worked to stifle it with her hand. "And I would be especially honored if you would let me worship you for the rest of our lives.

"You see," I continued. "It seems it's my life's purpose."

I opened the square wood box from the little antique store I'd been hiding for three months and presented her the ring I knew was perfect for her, even then. I'd replaced the center diamond with an emerald because she'd always told me that her grandmother's ring was just like that and how much she loved it.

"Will you marry me?" I asked, repeating the magazine's header.

"Yes," she barely whispered.

Zap.

THE END

WANT TO KNOW THE REST OF THOMAS & JANUARY'S STORY?
LISTEN TO THE GAMBLER BY FUN.

WWW.FISHERAMELIE.COM/NODYOURHEAD

Fisher Amelie is a member of The Paranormal Plumes Society.
http://theplumessociety.com/

ACKNOWLEDGEMENTS

Thank you to the editor who saved me. Hollie Westring, this book never would have been published without you. You didn't know it at the time but it's true. Plus, we're baby bump sisters. Sorry about *The Gambler*. Kind of. Sort of. Not really.

I'd like to thank my Plumes. Somehow being insane is cool and acceptable when I'm around you. Probably because you're all insane. That helps. So much love for you guys. When we're eighty, somehow I know we'll still be putt-putting around with each other, guilty of hijinks and blaming our age.

Thank you Petra Bagnardi. You're a modern day January with your multilingual skills. I seriously don't know how I would have done those translations without you. So grateful. Thank you, again.

And last because I always save the best for last. Thank you, hubs. I don't think talent like yours exists but in a select few and for damn good reason. Also, thanks for putting up with a messy house and dirty laundry. I know I always say that but I mean it. You're a trooper and I love you very much.

Made in the USA
Lexington, KY
16 May 2015